Tales From The Coast

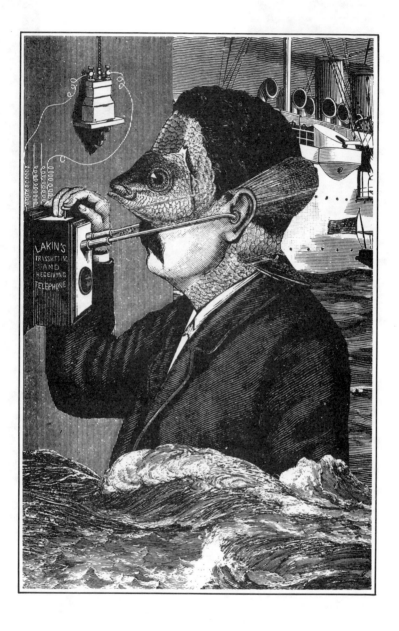

Tales From The Coast

Stories From The West Coast Magazine

Edited by
Kenny MacKenzie & Joe Murray

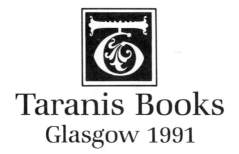

Taranis Books
Glasgow 1991

©individual authors 1991

typeset by Media Bridge

design by Alan Mason

published by Taranis Books*
Scenes From the Life No.23 and
Into the Roots by Janice Galloway
are published in her own collection **Blood**
by Secker and Warburg

printed in Gt. Britain by Bell & Bain Glasgow

ISBN 1-873899-00-9

*Taranis Books is an imprint of
MEDIA BRIDGE

Tales From The Coast

Stories from the
West Coast Magazine

West Coast Magazine is a quarterly publication produced in Glasgow since 1988. It specialises in new fiction and poetry, translations and short articles. The stories in this anthology all appeared in early editions of the magazine. Current editions and some back numbers are available at £2.00 from Media Bridge PO Box 849 Glasgow G31 2RH.

Contents

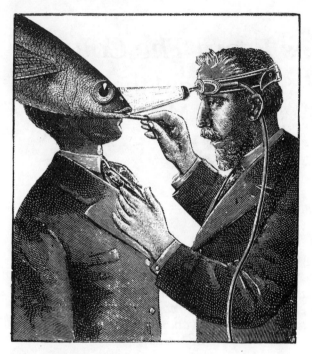

Arrival
Ronnie Smith

I remember the tension and excitement buzzing through our group as the guard announced our arrival at Beloostrov. Ilyich immediately abandoned his lecture to the soldiers who had scrambled on board at the Finnish border, and joined me at the window. The sun was beginning to rise above the flat white horizon and we could see only a formless human mass on the approaching platform. Ilyich elbowed me in the ribs and pointed to the small brass band which was surrounded by blood red banners, ornately embroidered with shining golden slogans.

"We're really bloody here now." The words leapt through his teeth which were clenched in a grin and I noticed that his chunky fists were closed tight. As the train came to a screeching halt we both rushed to the door, which was opened from the outside by a railway worker who looked up at us with puffing cheeks and staring eyes. The band blasted out a quick verse of the Marseillaise and then fell silent as a small delegation assembled before us. I recognised Ilyich's sister Maria first and then Kamenev, who looked thin after his Siberian holiday. Behind them lurked Koba, or Stalin as he now wished to be known. He hadn't allowed himself to lose any weight. Man of Steel indeed, block of wood more like. His only obvious talent was for robbing Georgian banks, in which Ilyich had given him every encouragement.

Kamenev raised his arms and smiled, first at us and then at the expectant crowd behind him.

"Comrades! It gives me the greatest pleasure to welcome comrade Lenin and our other comrades back to Russia. A Russia which has at last freed itself from the imperialist yoke. We look forward, comrade Lenin, to working side by side with you again in the struggle to build our revolution and to consolidate the historic gains which have already been made." The occasion was obviously far too solemn for him to throw in one of his tiresome jokes.

A loud cheer rose from the packed platform and a grey cloud of frozen breath hung in the air. The crowd surged towards us. Ilyich was lifted from the doorway and carried onto a rickety old table which had been pulled out from the waiting room. The soldiers all jumped from the train to hear his speech, with the exception of their young officer, who chose to lean in the carriage doorway smoking an English cigarette. Someone shouted from the platform suggesting that Krupskaya should also speak, but she declined on the grounds that her throat was too dry from all the excitement. Ilyich was always prepared to speak, all day if necessary. He smiled as everyone began to concentrate, to listen, to drink in the atmosphere and we took the opportunity to savour our first steps on home soil for many years.

I was glad to step onto soil of any kind as my bladder was close to bursting point and there wasn't even a bucket on the train. I found a quiet spot around the side of the waiting room, treading carefully to avoid plunging arse-high into a snowdrift.

Ilyich was stopped in full flow by the guard brandishing his watch and threatening to leave for Petrograd without us. So we had to scurry back to our carriage like errant schoolchildren as the crowd cheered us on. I was forced to struggle violently with my flies in order to catch up and in so doing two of the buttons popped off into the yellow stain in the snow. I had to abandon them and climb onto the carriage with the rest of the Bolshevik delegation.

As soon as the door was closed Ilyich turned angrily on Kamenev, his stubby index finger pointing at the unfortunate comrade's throat.

"What's this garbage you've been writing in Pravda? We got some back issues at the border and we were absolutely pissed-off reading your stinking, petty-minded editorials. I tell you, if I'd thought for one moment that you were going to start coming away with this shit, I'd never have appointed you to the board. That goes for you too Stalin."

Both their faces reddened. It was the first time I'd seen Stalin show any kind of emotion and I have to admit that I enjoyed the spectacle.

"I'm sorry Ilyich. But I don't quite understand." Kamenev floundered.

"I am only too well aware that you don't understand and I must assume that not one bloody member of the party in Petrograd understands either, since Pravda speaks in their name."

"Well, certainly the editorial Policy has been agreed by the board and none of the workers' or soldiers' delegates has voiced any opposition."

Ilyich turned to me, with his famous frustrated parent look.

"You see Grigory Evseyevich, the magnitude of the task we face? Within two weeks they've given our propaganda machine to Kerensky and his friends. And it'll take us months to get it back. You've been doing the bourgeoisie's job for them and I don't remember giving you instructions to that effect. Comrades."

His expression softened momentarily.

"Incidently, Kerensky and I were at school together. My father taught him."

Kamenev smiled. "Really? That is interesting. Now if we believe in fate..."

"But thankfully we don't." Ilyich snapped. "And so it is

not of any interest at all. Now come in here where we can talk. I want to bleed you dry of information. Grigory and I have a lot to catch up on."

As we followed him into an empty compartment I overheard Maria talking to Krupskaya, perhaps her voice was deliberately raised.

"Nothing's changed, I see."

Krupskaya was puzzled at first.

"What do you mean?"

"I mean that perhaps one day the women will also be taken into quiet corners and granted an audience. We just might have a larger contribution to make than typing letters and making the tea."

"Ah well, I hope you're not holding your breath Maria."

I quickly followed the others, cold stares nipped the back of my neck.

We talked for the rest of the journey as frozen snow fields and occasional dark woods drifted past the window. We were interrupted only by the rattling of the wheels as they ran over points. Ilyich appeared not to hear them. He shouted over the noise and insisted that we do the same, frowning like a child whose bed-time story is being read too slowly.

Ilyich hounded Kamenev and Stalin into giving us a detailed account of everything that had happened in Petrograd during the previous month. We pointed out their mistakes and explained our criticisms of Pravda's editorial line. They seemed quite offended. Understandable I suppose. After all we had just arrived while they had been in the thick of it, making practical decisions in the field. They must have resented our theorising from behind the lines. Too bad.

Stalin, as usual, said very little. Not committing himself until he knew who was going to win, always getting on my nerves.

Long after the sun had gone down we caught our first sight of Petrograd's lights. Ilyich's fists tightened again and he darted a quick, desperate glance at Kamenev.

"Do you think we'll be arrested at the station?"

Kamenev and Stalin burst into loud almost hysterical laughter.

Ilyich was first off the train. He neatly side-stepped the smiling group of comrades who were waiting to greet us. Instead they found themselves being led briskly back towards the main concourse by a man who had no time to shake hands. Kamenev and Stalin ran after them but I let them all go on ahead.

The station was crammed with people, soldiers, workers and party activists from every faction to the point where I was sure it would explode, hurling human debris all over the city. The entire building was festooned with red banners and everyone seemed to be wearing a broad red sash. A searchlight had been set up on a balcony and it swept the crowd, stoking up the already feverish atmosphere.

I could see at least a dozen bands blaring in harsh competition with each other and with the singing, chanting crowd. I had no idea what any of the bands was actually playing nor what the people were trying to say. The noise was simply an indistinguishable roar. As I watched the scene I realized that my mouth was hanging wide open.

Kamenev had stopped and was waiting for me half way down the platform with a serious look on his face, one eyebrow raised.

"Grigory, do you agree with what he said on the train?"

I knew he'd been desperate to ask me. "I don't know. We've only discussed these new ideas during the last few weeks. I'm not sure if I fully understand the direction he wants to take."

"I must be frank with you Grigory, from what I've heard to-day I think he's gone completely mad. It goes against every strand of Marxist theory, which he's always insisted comes first. And in practical terms his new tactics would lead us into a wilderness and destroy the party, just when things were shaping up."

"Yes I must admit that I almost agree with you.

However, the same things were said about him at the 1903 congress and we still followed him after that. He does make it all so interesting, we'd all be bored to death without all his ideological buggering about."

Kamenev laughed.

"Yes! What a tedious drudge revolution would be if we were in charge eh?"

Then he leaned over to speak quietly into my ear.

"By the way Grigory, your flies are undone. Did you know?"

"Yes I did know, I lost a few buttons at Beloostrov."

"I see. Perhaps you should fasten your overcoat."

We managed to catch up with the welcoming party, who had become utterly dishevelled. They had obviously made careful plans which Ilyich was refusing to adhere to. He was now in what used to be the Tsar's exclusive waiting room, clinging awkwardly to a massive bouquet of red roses. His path to the main exit was blocked and he shuffled his feet in boyish frustration. Chkheidze, the Menshevik President of the Petrograd Soviet, would not move. The pompous ass had a speech to deliver, a duty to perform. I was sorely tempted to squeeze my fingers around the pedant's throat.

"Comrade Lenin..." Even after just two words I noticed that his dull monotone hadn't changed over the years.

"... in the name of the Petrograd Soviet and of the whole revolution, we welcome you to Russia. But we consider that..."

"Oh piss off Chkheidze!" Ilyich hissed, "I promised myself the last time we met that I would never let you finish a speech again. Here, hold these."

Chkheidze gasped and spluttered behind the roses as everyone else followed Ilyich outside onto a balcony overlooking the wide station entrance.

The whole area was jam-packed with workers and soldiers, more bands and armoured cars with more search-lights. It was the scene which we had never dared to expect, our apparently triumphant entrance onto a stage we'd worked so hard to build.

I heard a gruff old voice from the past, "Ah ha! there's Zinoviev," and I felt my face flush with the warmth of childish pride. Then I heard other voices, just as gruff as the first. "Who the hell is this fellow Lenin? Its too bloody cold to be standing around here for him, whoever he is." I didn't know what to think, who were all these people anyway? Were they all members of our faction, were they even members of the party? How could they be? We were a spectacular minority, an elite.

Ilyich harboured no such doubts. He was obviously surprised at first by the size of the crowd but when one of the search-lights shone on his stocky frame, he composed himself with a deep breath.

"Dear comrades; soldiers, sailors and workers. I am happy to greet you in the victorious Russian revolution, to greet you as the advance guard of the international proletarian army..."

Krupskaya pulled lightly at my coat. It was the first time I'd seen her since Beloostrov.

"Can't we get out of here, Grigory? We'll be stuck all night if we wait with Ilyich and we've heard this bit before."

I nodded my agreement. She looked as exhausted as I felt, we needed some warmth and comfort after our journey.

A young Bolshevik had overheard us. "Excuse me comrades, I have the use of a car. It's on a side-street not far from here. I'll take you to the Kshesinskaya Palace if you like."

I was puzzled by this offer.

"And why will you take us there, comrade?"

"That is our new headquarters."

"So isn't the great ballerina there any more?"

"Oh her? No, I'm afraid she left in quite a hurry, comrade."

The three of us were still laughing as we finally squeezed our way to the edge of the straining crowd. Out in the dark empty side-streets it really felt like being on the margins of history.

At last we got into the car. The seats were very stiff and upright and in order to fit in beside Krupskaya I had to unbutton my coat. She immediately burst out laughing again.

"My god Grigory! Your flies are undone, don't you feel a draught?"

As we drove along the back of the crowd we could just see Ilyich's illuminated figure on the far-off balcony. Krupskaya was obviously enthralled, even at that distance. My greatest hope, at that moment, was that the ballerina had forgotten the sewing box in her desperate flight from the revolution.

God's Blessing At San Salinas
J. William Doswell

vita's brown eyes stared at the crucifix fastened to the adobe wall above her head. Kneeling beside the bed, elbows resting on the cornhusk mattress, she cradled her chin on old, thick veined hands. They were labourers' hands, nails broken and clotted with dirt. Lips barely moving, she said her prayers in slow Spanish whispers, the words making less sound than the wind in the palm fronds outside.

It was an old, plaster crucifix and the paint on the figure of Christ had faded. Her grandmother had given it to her when she had taken her first communion nearly sixty years before. It had been moved only once since then. When Evita married, she took it down from the wall of her room in her parents' house, had it blessed by father Donaldo, and hung it in this room, above the bed she was to share with Tomas. There it had hung for over forty years, prayed to at births, sicknesses, deaths, and for the many needs and dreams a person has in a lifetime. Even in a remote mountain village like San Salinas, hidden in the jungle of northern Nicaragua, a person has needs and wants that are beyond his own ability to provide, that require the dispensation of a gracious God.

Finished the prayer, she made the sign of the cross with precise movements and, with a grimace and faint sigh, pulled herself upright. One leg was shorter than the other and, as she crossed the room, she moved with an odd, dipping limp. The pain in her hip and leg was a constant reminder of the soldiers' nightmare visit to the village. But the real pain was carved in her mind and in her heart. She had prayed to the crucifix to be allowed to forget what had happened, but so far her prayers had not been answered.

She stopped before a rough, wooden chest, leaned her shoulder against it and worked it away from the wall. A tree lizard darted out from under the chest and scampered across the tamped dirt floor. It's tail jerked nervously as it sought a way out of the room. Normally she would have pursued it with a broom, sweeping it towards the doorway. But this morning her thoughts were elsewhere and she paid it no attention.

Feeling along the back of the chest with her fingers, she slid a piece of wood free and pulled some carefully folded bills from the cavity. Deliberately she laid the notes out by denomination in neat rows on top of the chest. It was her life's savings. She and Tomas had saved it together. After the soldiers killed him she had stopped. For her life had stopped. There was no future to save for. She counted the rows twice to make certain of the amount, for it was not something she did often and it was very important that she have the correct amount. She finally decided she had 640 and that relieved her greatly. The captain had said she would need 500 cordobas for *mordita*, the bite. She had known all her life that nothing was free, that you paid for everything, even the smallest favour. She was not angry at the captain for his extortion; she was excited by his offer.

She stacked 500 cordobas to one side and folded the remaining bills and returned them to the hiding place in the back of the chest. Then she pushed the chest back against the wall, erasing the marks it made on the dirt with her bare feet.

Going into the kitchen, she wrapped the money in a rag. Hoisting her loose-fitting dress, she hid it in her undergarments. She adjusted the packet, assuring herself it was secure and couldn't be seen. It was seven miles down the mountain to the army post and these days there were many bad people on the trail.

Stooping she pulled a water jug from under the table. Before the long trip she would water the flowers on the graves of her husband and son, and her son's wife. The soldiers had killed them all two years ago; only she and her grandson, Angel had escaped. He had run off into the jungle and she had not seen him since. The jug was heavy and she staggered as she lifted it and shuffled through the door into the dusty road. It was still early but the sun was already above the trees and she knew from the warmth on her head that the day would be hot.

The cemetery was across the road. Hacked from the jungle, the land had been cleared to accommodate the dead who were buried in a line parallel to the road. Everyone in the village had joined in the task; the dead had to be buried quickly because of the heat. The priest had come up from the valley and spent a busy day blessing the bodies. By the time he had finished repeating the funeral service so many times, God's words had been robbed of any individual application and Evita worried that her family had not been blessed. She still worried about it and prayed to the crucifix every day just to make sure God knew it was Tomas, and their son and their son's wife.

The three graves were near the end of the line of mounds. She had planted flowers in the shade and they formed a semi-circle around the wooden crosses she placed at their heads. She whitewashed the crosses often and kept the graves as neat as she did her home.

The cemetery became an extension to her home, an open-air living room separated by the road. She visited it each day, carrying on conversations with her dead family as though they were still alive. Evita knew some of her neighbours thought this was strange, but it did not bother her. Their's had been a close family in life. She saw nothing odd about continuing the relationship in death.

Eventually, the crucifix above her bed, the cemetery, and her church became the parameters of Evita's world and she did not speak, except to God and to the carefully tended graves. She talked to them about the same things they had talked about in life: the weather, crops, the war, and what to have for supper the next night. She could not provide them with gossip because she no longer talked to her neighbours. She was sorry about this because all of them had enjoyed discussing the other villagers' affairs. She knew they missed it and she tried to make up for it by speculating on what was happening. She exaggerated some times but felt no guilt. Didn't the cook sometimes thicken the broth?

Evenings were hardest on her. Evenings, the family had gathered at one house or the other and talked and laughed while the twilight deepened and gave way to night. Sometimes they drank a little cerveza. Then, Tomas forgot his age and when they got to bed tried to act like a young man. It had been a peaceful life; not exciting but fulfilling, a good life for a family to live.

"I am going down the mountain today," she told Tomas as she dipped water onto the flowers at the head of his grave. "That is why I am early. When I return, I'll have a surprise that will make you happy. No, don't try to worm it out of me, it's a surprise."

She finished watering, picked up the jug and recrossed the road. In the kitchen she wrapped six tortillas in a damp cloth and put them in a flour sack. It was a long way to the army post and back. She patted her loins to be sure the money packet was in place. She kneeled before the crucifix, her head bowed, hands folded before her. When she finished her prayers, she picked up the sack and left the house.

She met nobody on the road and made good time. Although the sun was hot, she did not think of the heat. Her mind was on the captain and his offer.

In the late morning she paused for water at a campesino's hut and ate two of the tortillas. She ate rapidly and did not linger. She wanted to get back before dark and share the surprise with her family.

As she neared the town where the army troops were stationed, she left the road and made water. For the first time in her life she did not fear the soldiers. They could not hurt her further. But, she did not trust her bladder; perhaps it was not as strong as her heart. Soldiers were like dogs, they feasted on fear. If her bladder voided, they would see a weak victim to pounce on and persecute. Perhaps, to kill. Then, she and her family in the graves on the mountain would be separated forever.

The captain knew she had arrived but kept her waiting for an hour while he ate his lunch. Evita did not mind. It gave her a chance to rest. She sat in the dirt in the shade of the low adobe building and listened to the cicadas hum their monotonous song. It was not far past midday. Even though the road home was uphill, she would be home before dark.

Finally the captain came to the door and looked at her. He continued to look at her while he picked his teeth, an arrogant impersonal appraisal. Spitting the tooth pick out, he beckoned to her and went inside.

Blinds were drawn against the sun and Evita stood just inside the door until her eyes adjusted. She was glad she had stopped in the bushes and emptied her bladder. She was afraid.

The captain was seated behind a desk, his chair propped against the wall. He eased it to an upright position and stared at her in the dim light.

"What is your name," he asked.

"Evita Herrera."

The captain looked at a piece of paper and made a mark on it. "Through there." He pointed to a door across the room. Tilting his chair back against the wall again, he dismissed her.

Evita opened the door with a mixture of apprehension and excitement. Perhaps she had built her hopes too high. Perhaps the captain was wrong. She shouldn't have told Tomas - what if there was no surprise?

The heads were arranged in rows like cabbages in a market. It was an awful sight to see human heads treated so casually. She stared in horror and in sadness and wondered how God could allow such a thing to happen. Surely, there could be no greater blasphemy.

It was close in the room and flies swarmed on the heads, their insistent buzzing the only sound. The sickly sweet smell of rotting meat hung heavy and she retched and bile rose in her throat. She crossed herself and covered her mouth and nose against the stench. Clutching the sack in one hand, she began inspecting the heads, searching for Angel. When she moved, she upset the flies and they darted around her, angry at being disturbed.

She found his head on the second table. She looked intently to make certain the mutilated head was Angel's. The eyes were closed and bruised and a gash, now covered with hardened blood, ran from the left ear to below the chin. But it was Angel. She was certain. Just above the nose, between the eyebrows, was a v-shaped scar, reminder of a childhood rock fight.

Putting the sack on the floor she raised her skirt and quickly took the money package from its hiding place in her undergarments. She thanked God the captain had remained in the other room and she had not had to do this in his sight. She opened the sack and, trembling, reached over and lifted Angel's head by the hair and put it into the sack. The flies rose and she reeled back, flailing them with her free hand. As she turned to the door, holding her breath against the smell, she prayed each of the heads had someone to claim it.

Evita hummed to herself as she left the army outpost. She was eager to get home and share her surprise. Tomas and their son and their son's wife would be so happy. The family was together again. Truly, God had blessed them.

The Collectors
Agnes Owens

Davey came up over the steep stony track that led to the golf course, once he had climbed a fence and crossed a burn. Every so often he stopped to catch his breath. He wasn't young, coming up for sixty and the rigours of a hard life had taken it's toll. When he reached the fence he came upon Tam Dugan sitting on a tree stump, his arms folded as if he had been patiently waiting on him.

"Saw ye comin' in the distance," said Tam with a jovial smile. "I thought I might as well get ye up."

"Aye," said Davey with a nod. He could hardly refuse the offer for Tam was a big strong looking fellow in his early twenties with a police record as long as his arm, mainly for assault and other things besides.

He climbed over the fence stiffly, then jumped the narrow burn with Tam following suit much more easily though.

"Up collectin' your golf-ba's?" said Tam. "I hear you dae quite well."

"No' bad," mumbled Davey, his voice lost in the wind that had sprung up carrying a drizzle of rain along with it.

He gave his companion a side-long glance wondering if he was as bad as folk said - it was easy to be in trouble nowadays, especially if you were young and had nothing to take up your time.

Tam turned round and said humbly, his coarse handsome face marred by a scar running the length of his left cheek, "I hope you don't mind me comin' alang wi' ye. I thought I might try some collectin' masel'."

"Why no?" said Davey. "It's a free country," though his heart sank.

He didn't want anyone poaching on his preserves - at least not alongside him. Admittedly there were others who collected golf-balls, solitary figures in the distance acting as if they were only out for a stroll and keeping well clear of each other.

"It's right cauld up here," said Tam, ducking his head from the wind and sticking his hands in the pockets of his flimsy black anorak.

"The higher you climb the caulder it gets." said Davey, himself being warm enough with his cloth cap on and wearing a Donkey jacket he had purchased from an ex-Youth Training Scheme employee.

He hung back a bit to pick up a golf-ball he had spied on the grass a few inches off the path. Tam looked round to say with surprise, "You've got wan already and we're naewhere near the course?"

"Ye can get the odd wan as far doon as the fermer's field but up the top beside the golf-course is the best place."

The words were hardly out of Davey's mouth when Tam was bounding on ahead.

"I hope he stays oot ma road," said Davey under his breath, taking his time in reaching the top and finding two golf-balls on the way up. When he got there Tam was standing not far from the path, his face a picture of misery. "Ma feet are soakin'," he said. "It's a bog here."

"Ah well," said Davey, regarding his own heavy wellingtons complacently, "You've got to put on the right gear for this business."

"How was I tae know?" said Tam, staring ahead in a

sullen manner at the long stretch of grass, moss and whinbushes parallel to the golf-course.

"You can always go back," said Davey.

"I might as well stay noo that I'm up here." said Tam walking on slowly. Then his long arm swooped down on the rough grass.

"A golf-ba'" he shouted, "A pure yellow wan tae. It's a beauty."

Davey came up to join him. "Very nice. A good make as well. You've done no' bad."

"No' bad! I've done better than you. This is pure yellow and you've only got a white one!"

"I've got three," said Davey tapping his pocket.

"Ye never telt me that," said Tam, looking put out. "How no'"

"Dae I have tae tell ye everythin'?" suddenly feeling fed up and wishing he had turned back when he first clapped eyes on this big pest.

Abruptly he veered off through the moss down towards a drainage ditch where he immediately found two balls under the water. His pleasure was lost when Tam called "Don't tell me you've got anither wan."

"Naw, two," Davey called back, deciding that he was going to try and ignore Tam's attitude as best as he could for there was no point in getting worked up about it. The guy was worse than bad - he was mentally retarded.

At the same time he was almost glad when five minutes later Tam found a ball within a clump of gorse cursing the needles pricking his hand as he pulled it out.

"Anither wan," he shouted, holding it up for Davey's inspection.

Thank God for that, thought Davey. When he was forced to study it, he noticed it was chipped. All he said to Tam was, "Aye, very good," with a false encouraging nod.

The wind died down and the rain became heavier. The view of the town below was blanked out with mist. Tam said to Davey, "This weather would sicken ye."

"Aye," replied Davey, thinking it wasn't the only thing. He added, "At least it keeps the golfers away." So far he had seen only three of them on the other side of the course and they appeared to be hurrying in the direction of the golf-club.

"Them!" said Tam contemptuously. "They want their heids examined."

By the time they were half-way along the edge of the course, Davey had found another three and Tam another one. Though Davey had actually kicked the one in Tam's direction when he wasn't looking, simply to keep his mouth shut. For a minute or two it did the trick then he began to complain again. "I'm soaked through," he said. "There's a hut no' far away," Davey told him. "We'll take a bit shelter and see whit happens."

Before they reached the hut Tam said in an urgent note, "Listen - how much dae ye get for golf-ba's?"

"How much?" said Davey, frowning thoughtfully. "Oh well, at the maist three for a pound."

"Is that a'?" said Tam looking offended. "I heard ye got a pound each."

"I don't know where ye heard that, but I've only ever got three for a pound."

"So you're tellin' me." said Tam, his voice heavy with sarcasm.

"As ye know yersel'," said Davey trying to keep his temper, "Stolen property loses hauf its value by the time it reaches a buyer."

"I bet I could get two quid for that yellow golf-ball any day," said Tam. He snapped his fingers in the air. "Jist like that."

"You try it then," said Davey thankful to be nearing the hut. He would take a rest, drink the can of super-lager he had in the back pocket of his trousers, then return home. He'd had enough of this fellow.

They entered the hut and sat on a bench against the back wall - Tam gingerly on the edge of it, as it was exceedingly damp - and Davey leaning back carelessly with his legs stretched out.

"It's as cauld and wet in here than whit it is ootside," said Tam.

Davey brought out his can of super-lager. He offered it to Tam. "Here, take a wee drap o' this. It might heat ye up."

"No thanks," said Tam with a look of disgust. "I canny go that stuff. It tastes like gnats piss."

"Maybe so," said Davey, "But ye get accustomed to the taste. Besides, it's the effect I'm efter."

"Whit effect?" sneered Tam, staring moodily through the wide open doorway of the hut. "I'd rather have a hauf-bottle o' Bells, or even a joint. Dae you know ther's mair effect wi' a joint than that stuff."

"I widny know," said Davey putting the can to his mouth and wishing he had another two to go with it, for there really wasn't much effect from one can when he came to think of it.

"How many golf-ba's did ye say ye had?" Tam suddenly asked.

"Er - eh, five." said Davey vaguely.

"So, I've got three and that makes eight. If we got anither two that would be ten. I know where I could sell them for a pound each and that would be a fiver tae you and a fiver tae me."

Davey took another pull at his can. Definitely there was no effect from it at all and there wouldn't likely to be with this blow-hard rabbiting on in his ear.

"I'm gaun hame shortly," he said. "I don't feel sae good."

"Haw -flyman," jibed Tam.

This really angered Davey. "Whit dae ye mean - flyman? I'm gaun hame and that's that."

"Aye, because you've got the maist ba's, that's how."

"So whit, if I have," said Davey, actually beginning to feel a slight hit off the lager, which only increased his anger. "I found them, didn't I?"

"That's only because you were lucky. I wis lookin' every bit as hard as you and soaked tae the skin intae the bargain. Look at ma trainers. They're ruined."

Davey continued to drink his lager while Tam paced up and down the mud floor of the hut, his face grim and determined. He stopped suddenly to point his fore-finger at Davey's face. "O.K. if you're no collectin' I want yer golf-ba's."

"You're no gettin' them," said Davey, his voice less strong than he had intended as Tam leaned over him and growled, "Haund them ower pal."

Davey's patience was broken. He flung the contents of his can straight at Tam's face, blinding him with lager.

"Ya auld bastard," roared Tam, wiping his eyes with the back of his hands, then unzipping the top of his anorak to wipe his neck as he wriggled about to ease his discomfort. "That lager's fuckin' frozen," he added in an anguished tone, "As if I'm no wet enough."

Eventually he calmed down and glared at Davey as if wondering how best to deal with him. At that point Davey said, "Ye can have the golf-ba's then." He took the golf-balls out from his pocket and flung them on the mud floor one by one, but only five of them. Tam looked down at the golf-balls like a dog distracted by a bone. Then he glared back at Davey, clenching his fists.

"Listen you," he began to say when a voice from the door-way spoke, "I say you fellows, have either of you seen a red golf- ball? I hit it in this direction and I'm damned if I can see it anywhere."

The speaker wore a short yellow oil-skin with its hood tied tightly under his chin. What could be seen of his face was fat and ruddy cheeked. He could have been any age between thirty and forty, and he was holding a golf-club. Tam turned and snarled, "Naw, we huveny," the rage still plain on his face.

The golfer's eyes narrowed when he saw the golf-balls lying on the mud. "You've been stealing our golf-balls, I see."

"We never stole them," said Tam. "We found them and they're oors."

The golfer laughed unpleasantly. "You can tell that to the manager for I'm going to report you as soon as I get back to the club."

"Report away," said Tam with an equally unpleasant laugh.

"In the meantime," said the golfer, "You can give me up those golf-balls and I might let you away with it this time. That is," he wagged an admonishing finger at Tam, "if I don't ever see either of you up here again."

He then addressed Davey, who had never moved off the bench, sitting with his empty can of lager in his hands and his legs crossed like a disinterested onlooker. "As for you, you're always up here pinching our golf-balls. You definitely should be reported."

He was about to say a lot more when Tam tapped him on the shoulder with a look of disbelief on his face and said, "Dae you mean to say ye want me tae bend doon and pick up these ba's and personally haund them ower tae you?"

"Exactly."

"That'll be right," said Tam as he began to kick them one by one under the bench. "If you want them get them yersel'."

"Right," said the golfer, his cheeks turning purple. "I will and you'll definitely be reported."

As he bent down to retrieve them Tam gave him a shove. The golfer landed flat on the mud, his nose barely missing the bench. Tam let out a guffaw of laughter.

"There wis nae need for that," said Davey, helping the golfer to his feet and making feeble attempts to wipe the mud off his chin. The golfer backed off outside the doorway shaking his fist. "Just wait," he shouted, "I'll be back with my mates. You've both had it. I can tell you." His voice became fainter as he vanished round the side of the hut.

"I soon got rid o' him," said Tam to Davey as if nothing amiss had happened between them. Then he froze and pointed outwards. "Christ, he's left his golf-club."

He picked it up and went outside to hit great chunks of moss into the air, calling to Davey, "This is a' right. I think I'll have a go roon the park wi' this club."

Davey placed his empty can under the bench and came out into the open. "We'd best get crackin' afore these golfers come back."

They were a good bit down the path when Tam said, "Christ, the golf-ba's. I forgot them," and ran back towards the hut.

Davey kept walking, hoping the golfers would meet up with Tam and beat him to a pulp. It didn't happen. Tam came back five minutes later, his pockets bulging. "Fancy forgetting them," he said laughing.

Davey looked behind. When he saw there was no one following he said to Tam, "You walk on. I canny keep up wi' ye."

"I'll walk slow," said Tam. "I came oot wi' ye. I might as well go back wi' ye." Then after a pause he reached into his pocket adding, "You can take four ba's back and that'll be four each. That's fair enough, isn't it?"

"Very fair," said Davey, just wanting to get rid of Tam at all costs. Tam went on, "Dae ye know whit I've been thinkin'?"

"Naw - whit?"

"I've been thinkin I'll gie ma golf-ba's and club to the young yins that hit golf-ba's roon the park. It's a bloody shame they canny afford tae play on a real course. Dae ye no' think it would be a nice gesture?"

"Very nice indeed," said Davey after picking up a red golf-ball half way down the path, which Tam didn't notice being so bemused with his thoughts.

They reached the fence and after they had climbed over it and were crossing the fields Tam said, "Dae ye know I enjoyed masel' the day. It's a great wee hobby collectin' golf-ba's. But the next time we go we should try that private course up at Lynmoor. We can always get the bus up. It's no that dear - " He broke off as Davey began to run - not very fast though because of his wellingtons for one thing and his age for another. Tam caught up with him easily. He said, "Whit's wrang wi' you. Are you in a huff or somethin'?"

Incident During The Circulation War
Alan Mason

It happened some years ago (said Riley) when I worked on *The Quartermaster,* a monthly magazine for boys. We were in the middle of a circulation war, and our Editor, old MacAllister, had been sent the draft of a new puzzle by Mr. Henry Deal, the acknowledged puzzle maker of the age. *The Quartermaster* insisted on having the best of everything - a requirement which, on this occasion, caused us something of a headache, for we suspected that the presence of the puzzle within our walls was known to a rival publication. While the puzzle remained in the Office we were obliged to do the same.

That said, I was happy enough to dine with MacAllister every night. He was, without a doubt, the steadiest fellow I have ever met; a veteran of the Zulu campaign, whose composure, when it came to cards, served increasingly to show my two companions in the worst possible light.

"What in the world induced you to lead that heart?"

"I did not know what to lead. The diamonds were obviously against us."

"Diamonds? Who said anything about diamonds? Could you not have led a black suit? You had a black suit of some kind, I suppose?"

"Yes, I had a black suit, and I've got it still - but I'm keeping that for your funeral."

The evening had progressed pleasantly enough (with, as yet, no resort to fisticuffs) when MacAllister, who had gone to his dressing-room to find change for a large coin, thought he heard, directly below, the sound of keys being thrust into the lock of the front door.

A minute later he returned to the card-table, looking, if anything, a little calmer than usual.

"You chaps," he said, putting on his coat, "it seems that someone is trying to force the front door. There is a light in the entrance hall. Shall we go down and watch the operations?"

Knowing him too well to take this for a joke, we laid aside our cards and followed him downstairs.

In the dim light of lowered gas, the four of us stood silently on the mat, holding our breath and listening to the man who worked on the other side of the door. There were no bolts to prevent an illegal entrance, merely a large lock and chain in one piece with the handle.

After trying several keys, the idea of opening the door by unlocking it was apparently abandoned. We looked at each other and smiled. Would our unwelcome visitor now depart, tail between legs? Presently, with a sound like a dog eating biscuits, the evil-looking point of a centre-bit emerged from the woodwork of the massive panel. MacAllister motioned us to stand aside, for it was only natural to suppose that an eye would be applied to the hole once completed. Owing to the thickness of the woodwork, the limit of vision through the aperture would be restricted: by crouching down, therefore, we easily made ourselves invisible.

A minute later we were hunched at the door, looking up at a hole the size of a saucer.

An idea struck me - a rare enough occurrence - and I crept back to the hat-stand, where a leather dog leash hung beside MacAllister's top hat. He gave a little nod as I drew the thong towards me; for he read thoughts as other men read print. I passed the noose end through the steel swivel, and, crawling on my knees to the door, lifted the loop and positioned it round the hole. I was just in time. The man outside had apparently delayed in order to turn up his sleeve. He was in no great hurry, I must say; and we wondered afterwards what had become of the special police guard that was meant to be guarding the Office.

A dirty hand - essentially the hand of toil - came through inside my slip knot. This was followed by a bare white arm. I felt inclined to laugh, and my two hands, outstretched to hold the dog leash in place, shook visibly. The elbow entered and curved, while the dirty fingers crept over the mechanism of the lock and chain with the assured touch of precise knowledge. A little further until the muscles of the upper arm were visible - then I drew the noose tight, cutting deep into the sinews. We pounced upon the arm, holding it tight against the woodwork while his fingers worked convulsively - drawing it through right up to the shoulder while I made fast the dog leash to the two bolts of the locker which jutted out at the top of the door.

"A neat job!" said MacAllister, as we stood back and contemplated the twitching white arm. "A very neat job indeed."

Leisurely he began to unchain the door.

I was of an athletic turn of mind in those days, and when I proposed opening the door, my colleagues stepped back and ceded to me the place of honour. I opened it with a jerk and thrust out my hand to where his throat must be.

But my fingers seemed to go right through it, and I grasped something that felt like a chain in a tangle of warm, wet seaweed ...

His companions had, for their own protection, cut the throat of this poor hired expert. They had done it so effectively that the head was only retained by the vertebral column. In his agony he had grabbed the bell with his right hand, and the rigid fingers still held to the handle.

He was crucified face foremost against the door.

I had clutched his spine.

The Silver Quoit
John Burns

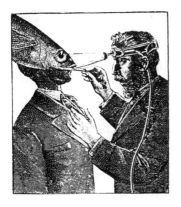

T am Buchanan was Rob's grandfather, a small wiry man of about sixty. Bald. Rob was only nine, but for him that was a long time, and for all that time his grandfather had been bald. He wore a bonnet like all the other men and Rob was fascinated by the way he would often push it back, scratch his head and say,"Aye," quiet-like, as if God had just let him into a secret. Something in this affected the boy deeply. It was part of a world to which he did not yet belong.

As Rob took his place between Iain and Hughie he glanced over to where Tam Buchanan stood having a smoke and a bit crack with Allan Murdoch. The quoiting-green was busy, and the still summer air was broken only by the village gossip, the sharp clink of quoit on quoit. Now and again a shout went up as someone landed right on the pin. But for Rob it wasn't these sharp, clean metallic sounds that held him, but the slap and suck of the heavy iron quoits as they fell on the clay beds and sliced into the torn scraps of newspaper used as markers.

The clay was gey queer stuff. Some days it was all hard and cracked and left white powdery marks on your clothes. On other days it was wet and grey and soggy. A favourite game was to roll the wet clay into smooth round marbles, then let them dry in the sun or in the oven so that they became as hard as cannon balls. Thrown at toy soldiers carefully placed on the banking of the quoiting-green they exploded and sent up clouds of dust just like in the war films at the pictures.

Once Rob had gone with his father and grandfather to Balgary where they had dug up the clay on the shore when the tide was out. It was put into sacks and taken back in the boot of the car to the village to replace the dried-out clay in the beds of the quoiting-green. It was heavy in the bags and Tam Buchanan swore a lot carrying it up to the car, but now it was safely bedded he swore less and concentrated more on the graceful arcing flight of his quoits, only muttering under his breath now and then if other quoits covered the pin making it hard to get a clear view of the target.

As the boys watched, Tam stepped up to take his throw. Rob knew he was good because he had seen the big silver cup on his granny's sideboard, and to a nine year old that was all that mattered - winning. The other men, however, appreciated the graceful rhythm and timing of the art, to say nothing of the unfailing accuracy. Shouts of encouragement rang out as Tam swung and sighted, swung and sighted, steadying the quoit briefly at the top of its swing to sight the pin or the paper markers before releasing it. The quoit rose high in the air before curving earthwards to land just to the right of the pin.

To the boys all this was a simple test of strength. They had all tried to throw their fathers' quoits and found it impossible. Two-handed they could pitch them a few feet, but they could never get them into the air. So they played with them, pressing them into the soft clay until they left an imprint of their shape, or filling up the holes on the flat side with clay that was then left to harden.

Rob was lucky. His grandfather had given him a wee silver quoit he had won somewhere. It was about five inches across and it was perfect in every detail, beautifully curved on the top with a cut-out for grip just like Tam's own quoits. It even had a sort of criss-cross scoring under this cut-out to give the hand a bit more grip. Last summer he had played nearly every day with this quoit but then he had mislaid it and had almost forgotten about it, though every so often he did remember and was rather embarrassed at not knowing where it was when his grandfather asked about it, as if it had been a sort of pact between them. It wasn't a toy. It was real. Tam Buchanan had given it to him because he was old enough to have a real quoit and to look after it. Somehow losing it seemed to show that he wasn't. He hated letting his grandfather down. Even more, he hated the idea that maybe the old man thought he just didn't care.

Tonight, though, wasn't a night for reflection. Tam Buchanan was on form. He had hit an easy flowing rhythm that would probably win the match. The boys knew this and soon lost interest because the end was now a foregone conclusion. While the rest of the spectators applauded Tam's performance, the boys wrestled up and down the steep banking which formed one side of the quoiting-green until they grew bored and decided to sneak up behind the summer seat where the village women were gossiping away. They were bound to hear something interesting there.

Rob lay on his back looking up at a clear blue sky. It was one of those long summer nights when the light seems to go on forever. It was strange lying there with the various sounds of the village all around him, but with nothing to be seen except the vivid blue of the sky, seared every so often by the black flashing arc of a swallow. Life was endless and bright as the sky.

The next morning Rob was sitting at his breakfast lazily reading the back of a cornflake packet and letting his mind wander over the day to come. He had half-planned an expedition with Hughie to the Billies' Cave, a damp, dark hole in the steep soggy banking of a burn that held an endless fascination for them despite the fact that neither of them was actually brave enough to go in. You had to wade in through the narrow opening, hunched over to keep away from the dripping ceiling, not letting on how nervous you were of the deeper shadow that marked the opening of another tunnel further on. They had never reached that opening, had always turned back and waded quickly back to the main entrance, to the rush of the burn, the scent of earth and trees and primroses, the dazzling blue lightning of a kingfisher.

His dad was just having a quick look at the *Daily Express* while waiting on the van to pick him up for work. His mother was singing as she pottered about through in the back kitchen. But in an instant everything changed.

His aunty ran in shouting to his father,"Oh, Bill, Bill. It's ma faither!" She was crying and her long dark hair which she normally kept in a tight bun only emphasised the pallor of her face. Rob was shocked to the core by her words and by the panic in her voice. He just sat there, his heart violently crushed inside him, struggling for breath, while his father and aunty hurried over to his grandfather's house. As they went out his mother came through and put her hand on his shoulder. Her face was white and her hand trembled a little.

"Don't worry, son. Your grandpa's had a wee turn, but he'll be all right. You'll see."

But it wasn't all right. Tam Buchanan died two hours later.

A few nights after the funeral, Rob lay on his bed staring up through the skylight. Life was as incomprehensible as the empty blackness between the stars. Just recently his grandfather had started to show him the major constellations: Cassiopeia, the Plough, Andromeda, the taut leaping figure of Orion the hunter. They had stood together in the darkness behind the house away from the streetlights and played their game; the old man helping the boy to find his way through the vastness of space. Now his guide was gone, the way ahead was uncertain.

Every day the school bus passed the cemetery, and every day Rob tried to pick out his grandfather's grave. The figure of Tam Buchanan was always in his mind. He could still hear him swearing under his breath as he lifted the bags of clay at Balgary, could still feel the strong grip of his hands as he showed Rob how to swing a quoit.

He remembered the wee silver quoit, remembered he had lost it. He hunted everywhere for it. Nothing else mattered now. It was all he had left. But hours later he still hadn't found it.

He stood in the gloom of his father's shed, staring blindly in front of him, his mind blank and numbed, until a bitter anger caught at him and he grabbed and punched at the pile of old newspapers lying on the bench. The grinning spiky-haired face of Oor Wullie laughed up at him from the floor of the shed.

"Bastard!" he shouted, and swept a tool bag off the bench, spilling pliers and chisels and screwdrivers.

Sobbing, he slid to the floor and stared at the gaping tool bag.

There, among the jubilee clips, the sweet-scented putty, and the tins of Imp fluxite, was a scratched and battered silver quoit.

Scenes From The Life No. 23: Paternal Advice
Janice Galloway

I t is a small room but quite cheery. There is an old-style armchair off to the left with floral stretch covers and a shiny flap of mismatching material for a cushion. Behind that, a dark fold-down table, folded down. On the left, a low table surmounted by a glass bowl cut in jaggy shapes, containing keys, fuses, one green apple and some buttons. Between these two is an orange rug and the fireplace. The fireplace is the focal point of the room. It has a wide surround of sand-coloured tiles and a prominent mantlepiece on which are displayed a china figurine, a small stag's head in brass, a football trophy and a very ornate, heavy wraught-metal clock. On the lower part of the surround are a poker and tongs with thistle tops and a matchbox. Right at the edge, a folded copy of *the Sunday Post* with *the Broons* visible on top. Behind the fireguard, the coals smoke with dross. The whole has the effect of calm and thoughtfulness. It is getting dark.

Place within this, the man **Sammy.** He is perched on the edge of the armchair with his knees spread apart and his weight forward, one elbow on each knee for balance. He sits for some time, fists pressing at his mouth as he rocks gently back and forth, back and forth. We can only just hear the sound of a radio from next door, and the odd muffled thump on the wall. More noticeable than either of these is the heavy tick of the clock.

Sammy exhales noisily. He appears to be mulling over some tricky problem. He is. But we are growing restless in the silence. Suddenly, too close, a noise like a radio tuning and we are in the thick of it.

> put it off long enough and it wasn't doing the boy any favours just kidology to make out it was just putting it off for himself more like no time to face it and get on with it right it was for the best after all and a father had to do his best by his boy even if it was hard even if he didnt want to bad father that shirked his responsibilities no bloody use to anybody the boy had to be learned right and learned right right from the word go right spare the rod cruel to be nobodys fool that sort of thing right christ tell us something we dont know

The man stands up abruptly, scowling.

> No argument it needed doing just playing myself here its HOW thats the thing thats the whole bloody thing is HOW needed to be sure about these things tricky things needed to be clear in your mind before you opened your mouth else just make an arse of the whole jingbang just fuck it up totally TOTALLY aye got to be careful only one go at it right had to get it across in a oner and he had to learn it get the message right first time right had to know what you were at every word every move or else

Sammy walks briskly to the window in obvious emotional agitation, bringing a dout from his right trouser pocket, then a box of matches. He inserts the dout offcentre between his lips, takes a match from the box, feels for the rough side and sparks the match blind. The cigarette stump lights in three very quick, short puffs and still his eyes are focussed on something we cannot see, outside the window in the middle distance. Up on tiptoes next, peering. Violent puffing. He shouts.

> BASTARDS! SPIKY-HEIDED BASTARDS. AD GIE THEM PUNK. WHAT DO THEY THINK THEY LOOK LIKE EH? JUST WHAT DO THEY THINK THEY'RE AT EH?

and he is stubbing the cigarette butt out on the sill, turning sharply, going back to the easy chair to resume his perch. He runs one hand grease-quick through his hair from forehead to the nape of his neck and taps his foot nervously.

> christs sake get a grip eh remember what youre supposed to be doing eh one think at a time TIME the time must be getting on. Get on with it. Hardly see the time now dark already. Right. Thats it then. That does it. Wee Sammy will be wondering what the hell is going on what his daddy is doing all this time

Sammy's eyes mist with sudden tears as the object of his sentimental contemplation appears in an oval clearing above the mans head. A thinks balloon. Inside, a small boy of about five or six years. He has ash-brown hair, needing cut, a thick fringe hanging into watery eyes that are rimmed pink as though from lack of sleep. It is **Wee Sammy**. The balloon expands. **Wee Sammy** in a smutty school shirt, open one button at the neck for better fit, and showing a tidemark ingrained on the inside. One cuff is frayed. The trousers are too big and are held up by a plastic snakebelt; badly hemmed over his sandshoes and saggy at the arse. He is slumped against the wall of what we presume to be the lobby. It is understandable his father is upset to think of him; he looks hellish. God knows how long the boy had been waiting there. The eyes, indeed the whole cast of the body suggest it may have been days. And still he waits as we watch.

Sammy clenches his eyes and the balloon vision pops. POP. Little lines radiate into the air to demonstrate with the word GONE in the middle, hazily. Then it melts too. The man makes a fist in his pocket but he speaks evenly,

RIGHT. MAKE YOUR BLOODY MIND UP TIME. RIGHT.

then springs to the door where he steadies himself, smooths his hair back with the palm of a hand and turns the doorknob gently. A barless *A* of light noses in from the lobby with an elongated shadow of the boy inside. The mans faces is taut, struggling to remember a smile shape. One hand still rests on the doornob, the other that brushed back his hair reaches forward an upturned cup, to the child outside. A gesture of encouragement.

Sammy: Come away in son.

The shadow shortens and the child enters, refocussing in the dim interior. The door clicks as his father closes it behind and the boy looks quickly over his shoulder. The man smiles more naturally now as if relaxing, and settles one hand awkwardly on the boy as they walk to the fireplace. Here, the man bobs down on his hunkers so his eyes are more at a level with his sons. **Wee Sammy's** eyes are bland. He suspects nothing. The man has seen this too and throughout the exchange to come, is careful: his manner is craftedly diffident, suffused with stifled anguish and an edge of genuine affection.
(pause)

Sammy: Well. Youre getting to be the big man now eh? Did your mammy say anything to you about me wanting to see you? About what it was about?

Wee Sammy: (silence)

Sammy: Naw. Did she no, son? Eh. Well. Its to do with you getting so big now, starting at the school and that. You like the school?

Wee Sammy: (silence)

Sammy: Daft question eh? I didnt like it much either son. Bit of a waster, your da. Sorry now, all right. They said to me at the time I would be, telled me for my own good and I didnt listen. You'll see they said. Thought they were talkin rubbish. What did I know eh? Nothin. Sum total, nothin. Too late though! Ach, we're all the same. Anyway, whats this your das tryin to say, youll be thinkin. Eh. Whats he sayin to me. Am I right?

Wee Sammy: (silence)

Sammy: Why doesnt he get on with it, is that what your thinkin eh? Well this is me gettin on with it as fast as I can son. Its somethin I have to explain to you. Because I'm your daddy and because youre at the school and everythin. Makin your own way with new people. Fightin your own battles. Im tryin to make sure I do it right son. Its like I was sayin about the school as well, about telling you somethin for your own good. But I'm hopin you'll no be like me, that you'll listen right. And thats why I'm tellin you now. Now youre the big man but not too big to tell your old daddy he's daft. Eh wee man?

Sammy rumples his son's hair proudly. **Wee Sammy** smiles. This response has an instantly calming effect on the man and he raises himself up to his full height again. His voice needs to expand now to reach down to the boy. His demeanour is altogether more assured and confident.

Sammy: Ok. Thats the boy. Ready? One two three go.

Wee Sammy remains silent but nods up smiling at his father as **Sammy** pushes his hands under the boys oxters and lifts him up to near eye-level with himself.

Sammy: Up up you come. Hooa! Nearly too heavy for me now. Youre the big fella right enough! Now. Heres a seat for you. No be a minute, then up on your feet.

He places his son on the mantlepiece between the brass ornament and the clock. He shifts the clock away to the low table, pats some stooriness off the shelf with the flat of his hand, then lifts the boy high, arms at full stretch, to reposition him in the centre of the mantlepiece in place of the clock. The boy is fully upright on the mantlepiece.

Sammy: Upsadaisy! Up we go!

Wee Sammy: Dad!

Sammy: What? What is it son? Not to take my hands away? Och silly! Youre fine. On you come, stand up right, straighten your legs. Would I let you fall? Eh? Thats my wee man, thats it. See? Higher than me now, nearly up to the ceiling. OK? Now, are you listening to me? Listen hard I want you to do somethin for me. Will you do somthin for me? Will ye son? Show me you're no feart to jump eh? Jump. Jump down and I'll catch you.

There is a long pause. The man is staring intently into the child's eyes and the child's eyes search back. He is still tall on the mantlepiece among the china and brass ornaments, back and hand flat against the wallpaper flora. The man's eyes shine.

Sammy: Show your daddy you're no feart son. I'll catch
you. Dont be feart, this is your da talkin to you.
Come on. For me. Jump and I'll catch you. Dont
be scared. Sammy, son, I'm waiting I'm ready.

A few more seconds of tense silence click out of the
clock. **Wee Sammy** blinks. His hands lift from the wall and
he decides; one breath and he throws himself from the
screaming height of the sill. In the same second, **Sammy**
skirts to the side. The boy crashes lumpily into the tiles of
the fire surround. His father sighs and averts his eyes.

Sammy: Let that be a lesson to you son. Trust nae cunt.

Old Ralph
John Cunningham

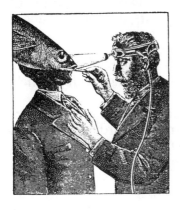

A tap running?

He put his hands on the side of the chair and raised himself. Standing fully up, an urgent pain in the bladder. He lifted his stick and made it to the toilet, parted the front of his trousers and let go a dribble.

All taps off. His breakfast cup was upturned by the sink in the kitchen hole. This was his domain. The room, the bathroom, the kitchen hole. The tap, dripping or running, a faint noise, was someone else's.

Snow improved the strict garden, except where the Warden had swept it off the steps and shovelled a path to the gate. His own foot-steps and stick-marks struck off from the path to and from the bird table. At 11 o'clock he'd gone out, after the Warden although not so soon as to seem to have been waiting, in the short blue rubber boots, and bits of snow had fallen in among his socks.

The birds had worried the bread off their table, and it

was scattered over the snow.

He looked left, willing Sonya to appear.

But only old Mrs somebody from the ground floor came into view, with a shopping bag. Crawling along in her silly fur boots, so bloody humble, asking to fall and show her knickers, be lifted off the ice by two great brutes of ambulance men. And it'll be poor Mrs, did you hear about Mrs, whatever her name, silly old bag.

Sonya walking when she was a child, with a basket of brambles, faint swirls of child-hair on her brown legs. And me hooking down brambles from the hedge with my stick. I was quite handsome - quite handsome.

He glared at the street and returned to his chair; rubber-ended stick against the arm, grey cardigan buttoned, fine wool scarf round clean collar and tie, handkerchief in the breast pocket, almost transparent hands on the arm rests. The central heating hummed.

We'd make a bronze, the chair and me, trousers descending into a sea of bronze. Bodily needs evaded. Solid and heavy in the dusk, people putting out their lights, extinguishing the blocks of golden falling snow ... their soft damp bodies to bed.

Where is she? He went to the kitchen and levered a biscuit from the pack, pushing his polished fingernail against the outside to raise a side of the top one, lifting it with the least possible crumbs.

Potatoes were peeled, broccoli spears washed, chops trimmed, a bottle of sherry in the cupboard and he wondered if she'd bring wine - a fruity Graves unrolling from tissue paper, greengold wine, Sonya turning, corkscrew worming, sigh of released wine; bottle on the table, colour in the glass! Soon, blurry disagreeableness from the gut.

But the first sip!

He went down to the window, was overheated on the side of his face next to the double-glazing, eating the biscuit.

She'd come up by train and caught a bus from the station. The Home was near the bus stop. A quiet part of town. The garden, where they'd sat by the bird table in summer, was smaller under snow.

Christmas tinsel draped the windows and his pale face watched from the undecorated one. She hurried through the hall, up shallow stairs, along thick linoleum.

- My dear Sonya!

Smell of aftershave, and hair oil. She liked this preservation of himself, confirming her own. She detached herself and went before him into the room.

I put the tatties on when I saw you coming! You're ravishing!

He took her coat, made her sit. Isn't she just! I can't have enough of her face, and eyes, and smile. My brambler's ripened!

I'm struck dumb by your beauty and haven't said a word! Sherry?

Both liked high-cheekboned, long nosed looks, and she had them. She filled the room. She was in the sherry cupboard. She filled the room with swirls of delight.

Keeping his head, he lit the grill and prepared the meat. Salt, pepper, a dab of butter on each chop.

From her chair the room was the same. The bed, curtained off; two prints on the wall, a desk, a framed photograph. Savings of a room-to-room, job-to-job life. You'd never known what next. Could have ended under a bush in the park. The scraggy skin on his neck, baleful eye, quick tongue; she relished his bitterness - loved him, and saw him twice a year.

He returned with drinks and got into his chair, hiding the shakes. He was looking at her legs with his gull stare; it used to make her uncomfortable till she discovered that it was his defence.

She crossed her legs. Slim. He'd no time for sausages hinged at the knee. When rare generosity made him admit that a woman with sausage legs was not bad he called her a nice person-grandperson-sweetypie-anything meaning cuddlyness other than of the flesh.

But here's Sonya.

They sit quietly, she with lowered head, Ralph erect, still as the bronze. The room is settling. Particles of air fall, taking the shape of table, desk, Sonya; become them as slowly and quickly as melted toffee, falling and hardening.

A beginning. I won't spoil it by talking.

There are grey hairs on top of her head. After a moment I'm not shocked. They're as sweet as the drying edges of a rose petal curled back from full bloom. Lovely. She touched my leg with her foot. We sit, go on sitting.

In a while I go to the kitchen, turn the chops, put on the broccoli, prod the spuds. She wasn't pitying me with her foot. Couldn't, any more than the birds out there, she's like them.

-Sonya? Are you hungry? The greens will be ready in a minute.

I know I'm shouting.

-Shall I set the table?

-Bless you dear, the things are in here, I keep them in here. And I'm handing them out to her. She knew they were in here, of course. Out of breath, gobbling like a turkey, my old wattles shaking. Think I've judged it right. Chops? Yes. Tatties dry and floury. The earwig in the broccoli water can go down the sink, but *extract* of earwig's beneficial. Earwig juice? Earwig water? No earwig, but I'll enjoy her pretending to be shocked. Then I must stop.

The warm plates. She's through there waiting to be surprised.

-A simple lunch, I thought you'd like that. He put it before her, with a jar of mint jelly.

-Oh, Ralph!

It had been the same last time; the time before that and every time. She'd have been troubled if he'd cooked anything else.

-Yes! Lamb chop from Flockharts! Have one every Sunday. My only treat and I buy the best. Superb butcher, you know what I mean? Hangs his meat and cares for it, one of the old sort. And he always keeps this back for me. Delicious, isn't it.

-And beautifully cooked. She dug in and enjoyed it.

Then ... a stream of grease was running down his chin and congealing, and he didn't know. She frowned.

This isn't criticsm, I wouldn't. Call it observation. But she's not as happy as when she came. Maybe I've said something. Maybe she'll get over it by making me amuse her. Yes, I'll be brilliant, curl her round in the palm of my hand like a little, snug little something-or-other. She'll be happy again, why shouldn't she? Otherwise I'll start to think of the cup of tea after she's gone. I won't think of it, I won't.

We're eating together. No need to talk. The fuss in my head, making it throb, I'll let down. Here are my shoulders up round my ears, let them down. And the other's finished, old man's lust. Must, bust, dust. Elephants have must. It's a must for them. His must is bust. Mind you, she can't help exciting it by the way she walks; can't walk down the street, bag of groceries, without spreading a scent, she walks in my dreams and I smell her ... that's to say, something passes from her to me.

From me to her, I hope. Damn, it's been passing between us while I've been gabbling to myself!

She's eating like a child, cutting the broccoli neatly as if she likes it but has been told to finish, and must pretend. She's gold and warm against the grey outside the window behind her head. We might be travelling through the landscape in a train. She's put down her knife and fork and looks at me. I'll go, she says, laughing. Enters the kitchen with the walk I was right about, returns with bread. She's always wiped her plate with bread. It means good health, contentment, and spreads to me. The height of bliss. Cheese? I ask, as if we met once a week.

-Ralph, I couldn't.

She has made a devilish quick change.

-I've brought you a present, she goes on.

How could she! It's square, wrapped, tied with curls of ribbon. Please not something home-made. Not what the children have made. Not personal or lasting, for me nearly dead. What we can destroy at once. Sweets, I hope it's sweeties!

He took a flat penknife from his pocket, opened its small blade and slit the ribbon. Took out a silver foil parcel - a pack of ground coffee - and turned it in his hands.

-Oh. But my dear, I haven't a -

-You only need a jug. I'll make it. Open and smell. She went to the kitchen, glimpsed the street and wondered how she was going to get back out there.

She'll soon be away. Coffee marks the end. He went through and stood beside her.

-Boiling water in the jug till it's hot right through, she demonstrated. Pour it back in the kettle. Four spoons of coffee in the jug, for the two of us. Water boils again, pour it in. Stir and leave five minutes. She led him back to the chair.

-We have this dinner (he was telling her about Christmas). I got sloshed.

-Oh Ralph!

-This dinner, I tell you. All very nice and so on. I took a cake, they expect something. We ate it wearing our paper hats, very jolly. Well anyway, with the turkey - I dropped a hint and I'm pleased to say they got it from Flockhart - we had sprouts. It was after that: when we were having a walk about and they were going to the loo and all that, I met May - rather a sweety-pie - and she says, did you like the dinner Ralph, and I said, wonderful May, except the sprouts, cooked to death, and she said, I did them. What could I do? Got pissed as a newt.

-Maybe she thought you'd had too much.

-I got drunk *after*, with my paper hat on! Oh yes I did... And then at New Year I took along her favorite sweet sherry, took it along to her room, revolting stuff. Still, we drank some of it. I needed absolution but she didn't give it me, the bitch. Hung onto her advantage.

Sonya slid to the floor and put her head on his knee.

-I've always hoped when I got to your age I wouldn't do anything silly.

He leant back; head would be tilted, eyes shut.

-Sometimes you have to try harder! Huh! A meals-on-wheels lady came the other day. Very nice woman. I told her about the parrot that laid square eggs. D'you know, she wouldn't be insulted?

-She was a nice person.

-I'm a horrible old brute.

She held his knee. If she could start again from the moment she entered, though it would again have been hopeless. After a while she pulled herself up and brought them two cups of coffee. And she was sitting on the chair, at the table.

She was talking about the children, her husband, it was tedious. She suggested he stay with them in summer as he used to.

There was nothing to do but join in. How were the children? The dogs and the cats and the rabbit? How was the farm? When would be a good time? It would be wonderful! They looked forward, though back. They thought about a date, and she looked in her diary. Train times were guessed. He'd take a taxi to Central and at the other end she'd meet him on the platform - where each imagined the meeting. He'd stay as long as he liked. They'd have walks in the hills.

I wish she'd go.

-Heavens, look at the time!

I don't want her to go.

-Must you really? Well, your coat.

Soft and warm, I settle it, on her shoulders. A quick brush of her lips to my cheek. Feet and eyes twinkle down the stair. She'll wave from the street.

Yes, a wave. And she gets out of sight as fast as she can, knowing what an old toad she has left.

I'll have tea. Wrap up. Go to the pub. Celebrate - bloody celebrate!

The Hunting of God
Angus Dunn

Extract from the Interim Report of the Emergency Committee Grangemouth Area

Headline from **The Sunday Sport**
Grangemouth Vanishes in 5-D Giant Boob Horror

Extract from **Peebles Advertiser and Herald**
Mrs Helen Gray (35) was cycling to work yesterday when her cycle suddenly turned into a crayfish. "It was ever so strange. One moment I was sitting on my saddle, the next moment it was a thing like a lobster!"

But the ordeal of this attractive blonde young mother of two was far from over. "I didn't even have a bag to put it in! And when I explained the situation to passers-by, they just didn't want to know!" Brave Helen wrapped the crayfish up in her raincoat and carried it home!

Document A

Statement of Mr. Alick MacRae, Elder of the First Reformed and Ancient Presbyterian Church, Barlogie, Perth.

On September 27th, last year, during our evening worship, God disappeared from the church. The minister, being a quick thinking man, called for the singing of the 27th metric psalm, and sent round the collection plates for the second time. This caused some confusion, and the service was hastily concluded before the congregation had fully realised what had happened.

Of course we called an emergency session of the church elders, (refreshments provided as usual by Mistress MacKay: and it was well up to her usual standard). Nothing like this had ever happened before, and we took some time to decide how to deal with the matter.

Finally, we called in the minister and explained our proposed course of action. We had decided that a suitable person should go and find God. The minister, a young man called Gillespie, agreed that this seemed the soundest approach.

Being men of substance in the community, the elders were unfortunately unable to undertake the task, and we informed Rev. Gillespie that we had agreed that he was the best man for the job. Nor would the congregation lose by the arrangement. Another minister would be engaged temporarily until Gillespie returned.

He then asked a question which gave pause to every member of the assembly.

"And how will I find God?"

We had a long discussion on this point, and it was finally decided that he should look for the Hand of God in all things, and this would lead him to the Lord. We were pleased to have found a formula with a suitably Biblical ring.

Gillespie left the next day and we did not see him for many months.

Document B

The Notebooks of Rev. Gillespie, Barlogie, Perth. (As the notebooks are extensive, often trivial and increasingly bizarre, extracts only will be presented in this precis.)

For the first few weeks of the august duty laid on me by the elders of the First Reformed and Ancient Presbyterian Church of Barlogie, Perth, I had no success. My appointed task seemed beyond my capacities. I grew morose, doubts began to assail me, and I began to feel that I must return to Barlogie and admit myself a failure.

I was residing in a respectable lodging house in Corstorphine at the time, and I spent the evening composing a letter of resignation. I went to bed that night in a mood of great despondency, my despair such that I could barely say my evening prayers.

Arising the next morning, I was taking a simple breakfast in the dining room, when I suddenly became assured that I had seen the hand of God at work. This I will enter in my notebook as item No. 1.

I am happy to relate that having once seen His Hand, like a man picking berries I began to see It everywhere, and this greatly encouraged me in my task.

No.1 The sun rose.

No.5 Mrs Harrison, my landlady in Corstorphine, was a woman of unswerving rectitude and unmitigated, though just, severity. She was hanging out her washing. A small boy leapt over a hedge, landing feet first in her basket. Two boys and a girl, who had been chasing him, hung over the hedge sniggering, waiting for him to be chastised.

Mrs Harrison grabbed the small boy and raised a hand to strike. As the hand descended, it entangled some undergarments hanging on the line. The hand, its force spent, descended gently, neatly depositing the undergarments on the boy's head.

Seeing what she had done, Mrs Harrison first gaped, then laughed uproariously. "Get away with you." she said, and let the boy escape.

No.15 Sauchiehall Street, Glasgow. I was standing in a shop doorway watching the passing throng for further signs of the Lord. I was feeling rather uncomfortable and conspicuous in my severe clerical garments.

I had almost given up, and was about to leave when I perceived an intoxicated man making his way along the pavement. Should I step out, our paths would inevitably cross. To avoid this meeting I remained in the doorway.

A look of panic came over the man's face, and he turned towards the doorway in which I was standing. He bent over convulsively, and I realised with horror that he was about to vomit on my feet. He glanced upwards, then turned 90 degrees, and vomited in the other corner of the doorway. He wiped his eyes and looked up at me again. "When I saw thon strange light about yer heid" he said, "I just couldnae throw up on yer shoes."

No.39 A strange tree on the moor touched by lightning.

No.57 Water pouring down a small cliff by the roadside. I touch the stone, it is wet.

No.90 The heron spread its wings, picked up its legs and glided off downstream.

No.128 I am staying in a communal house in a large city. I sleep in the kitchen.

Early this morning Janus staggered in looking for a cup of coffee. He was obviously suffering from the effects of the drink he took last night.

The coffee pot was in the sink, along with two days dishes. He swore, and pulled out the plug, letting the cold water drain out.

His upper lip curled. He kicked the nearest chair leg, muttering as he began to sort the plates from the bowls from the mugs from the cutlery.......

Hot water was run into the sink, and hands were plunged into the water that was too hot. Muttering and cursing continued as the first plates were laid in rows in the rack, as the broken mug was picked up from the floor and the cutlery was dumped into the sink tidy.

The last saucepan was the worst. Something had been burnt in it, several days ago. Janus laboured over it for some time, scraping the last of the carbon out of the corner.

The plug came out, the suds swirled away. He ran some more hot water into the sink, and rinsed it clean.

"Howzat!" he specified, waving a finger didactically at a sparrow in the garden.

He turned to me, where I lay in a sleeping bag on the floor. He grinned. "The world is all right."

No.135 The grain in a walnut burr.

No.143 Last night I sang as we sat around a fire. It was not completely tuneless.

No.157 The baby falls from the breast, almost instantly into a doze, warm milk on the pink mouth.

Before sleep comes, however, there is a moment of almost supernatural contentment which is neither self absorbed, as in sleep, nor outwardly absorbed, as when suckling.

No.185 The salmon leapt, everything urging it onward, upward.

No.201 The sun came up again.

No.235 Something dark happened under a tree, among the roots of a hawthorn. A long time ago. I survived whatever it was.

No.352 I can do it, muttered the old man. He glanced up and down the road, no-one coming. He jumped the ditch, hooking his cane in the fence to keep his balance. The brambles were ripe. The rusty fence began to give way, he leaned further and further back, there was nothing to hold onto except the thorny branches of the bramble bush. The muddy ditch beckoned.

As the fence gives way, the old man picks another bramble. How delicious they are!

No.465 The Goddess Demeter is unrelievedly sombre in the search for Her lost child. The woman of the household in which She takes shelter rebukes Her by exposing her private parts to the Goddess, at which she is so delighted that She blesses the house and family.

No.530 A slug creeps down a damp plank, racing the rising sun to the cool damp grass and the dark places.

No.680 My father's trousers were very patriarchal. A tweed that spoke of security and comfort, with a rich and pleasant tone of sternness.

He burnt them, one New Year's Eve.

He, a teetotaller, came home drunk and stood too close to the fire while jovially insisting that he'd had no more than a nip or two, and was by no means intoxicated.

No.811 A dung beetle rolls its ball across the hot plain, searching for a shady spot where it can mature.

No.1026 The sudden intrusion of God into otherwise pleasant circumstances.

No.1243 In the family rooms above a small draper's shop, a young Gujarati girl goes through the chore of buttering the family lingam. Suddenly she understands, and blushing, she glances around self-consciously to see if anyone is watching her perform this normally mundane act.

No.1598 A Greek man, old, but with the wrinkled face of a boy, cruel and thoughtless, and scarcely human.

No.1602 The salmon leaps, again. This time.......

No.1734 Suddenly, God.

No.2011. . . . .

No.2103 There are byways of the mind too bizarre to be wordable.

The moment before sleep, the extremes of intoxication, the opium haze of those in utmost pain or otherwise stretched to a limit.

That moment when a bird elides properly and logically into a bicycle. The understanding of what has just occurred, as it becomes a crayfish which is suddenly aware. It describes the happening to itself. This becomes the sweep of a brush on a mirror, and is gone.

No.2113 From out of the fifth dimension, emerged a breast: perfectly rounded, beautiful, its skin as smooth as eucalyptus bark.

Grangemouth lay in an evening fug of diesel fumes, refinery fumes, car fumes, and cigarette smoke.

The breast moved onward relentlessly, its warmth, and its all pervasive ambience, invading and dulling the senses of any who might have been watchful for this moment.

The breast from the fifth dimension languidly absorbed Grangemouth, then it turned, possibly looking for further nourishment. At that moment God, green-skinned and awesome, appeared in its path.

With one Hand, He stopped the breast in its path. His other Hand was raised on high. Then, poised ready to utter a terrible banishment, He looked at the breast, and thought for a moment about Grangemouth.

His shoulders shrugged. He bowed at the Waist, kissed the breast lightly, and vanished.

The last note in Gillespie's notebook is **No. 2113** *Shortly after this entry, he returned to Barlogie. There, he attended a meeting of the elders of the Church, and we were able to obtain a statement from one of those present at the meeting.*

Document C

Statement of Rev. Charles Ogden, Minister of the First Reformed and Ancient Presbyterian Church, Barlogie, Perth.

When Rev. Gillespie left on his special task, I was appointed temporary minister at Barlogie church. I feel I should point out that the elders at the very beginning told me about the inexplicable disappearance of the Divine Being, and I assured them that I would carry out my duties to the best of my abilities. I think I may flatter myself that the congregation has not felt deprived.

We would be disappointed, of course, if the Lord never returned, but without belittling His role in the life of the church, I think I can safely say that we would soldier on.

Despite my temporary status, I had begun to feel as if the church was truly mine, and I was gratified when the elders invited me to be present at the meeting when Rev. Gillespie returned.

Well. The meeting.

First of all, Rev. Gillespie appeared in the most unsuitable clothes, which did not please the elders, and made a rather poor impression on me - never having met the man before.

On being asked if he wished to retire to the manse to dress properly, he said that he didn't feel the cold anymore, and found the loincloth a very comfortable garment. However, as he was reporting in his capacity as minister of the church, he would of course wear his stiff collar.

His report was over three hours long and it ranged from the banal to the blasphemous. He compelled us to listen to all of it, even singing some parts! One of his so-called "Notes on the Presence of God" consisted of a silence four minutes and twenty- five seconds long, which he insisted we all join in. When one of the elders coughed, we had to start again!

From his notes and his manner it had become quite evident by now that Rev. Gillespie was no longer fit for his post, but I did not feel able to speak out. Even the elders were agitated, and at last Mr. MacRae took it on himself to tackle Gillespie.

"Please take a seat," he began.

"Thank you, I am quite comfortable as I am."

"Then please, at least stand!" Poor Mr. MacRae was quite distressed. It is unnerving to address a man who is sitting unsupported in the air.

Rev. Gillespie put his feet down, and Mr. MacRae continued. "It is evident that you have been through a lot in the last few months," he began tactfully, "and I dare say you could do with a rest."

"Not at all, I am ready to start again right away." Faces fell around the table. "In fact, I just stopped in to give you an interim report, and I must be on my way again."

"On your way?" Relief and confusion were mixed in Mr. MacRae's voice. "Where to?"

"Well, I have found lots of clues to His presence, but He's always gone before I can ask Him why He vanished from Barlogie Church. So I'm going to have a good look in the fifth dimension. It's a very strange place, but there's lots of traces of Him there.

"I'd better go now, but never fear;" he smiled and sudden light filled the room, "I haven't caught the bugger yet, but I'm on His trail!"

Then he vanished, and no one has seen him since. I am not looking forward to his next report.

Orr
Derek Steel

It's been a whole year now. Autumn; falling leaves, the plough out on the hill; and winter, sleet driven in against the four black panes of the window and running down the glass like slow tears. A bitter spring which brought the brief bleatings of lambs and terrible visions of flowers to my darkened room. Then long relentless summer days at the window, the ache of the empty fields outside, and nights clouded with soft murmuring wings, long without sleep.

Now another autumn; the swish of falling grain, and smoke from dying fires in the sky.

Last autumn I was out on the hill with the tractor, ploughing a straight furrow up and down. I turned at the top and the wheel went over a big rock. The brute overturned and rolled on me like a horse. My legs were crushed. I remember the earth smell, the reek of diesel, the terrible pressing on my legs, the screaming of gulls that were following the ploughing in a white plume over my shoulder. I covered my eyes from them as I lay in the earth beside the tractor. I have seen their lust for living eyes before.

It was she who found me. She noticed the ploughing had stopped and came up to see what was wrong. She took one look at me and turned and left again. To the birds, I thought. But she came back and covered me with blankets.

I could see the pale oval of her face, and then the sky, filled with a dying light. There were lines around her eyes I'd never seen. I remember her eyes, like dark wounds in a waxen mask. She never spoke, and shed no tears. The ambulance came after it was dark. I remember there was an owl in the beech trees at the top of the hill. But never a word, never a tear.

Only a month had passed when I began to notice Orr coming round. First his damned boots on the stones outside, then he would come in and gloat at me for as long as I could stand it, before going off to the kitchen. She would give him tea and scones, and he would sit by the Rayburn with his boots off. Soon he was coming regularly. I heard him and his damned boots every time. He didn't even bother to keep quiet after a while and he soon stopped pretending he'd come to see me.

I know how it happened. First there would be accidental caresses. I could sense the brief touching of hands, the electricity of skins. Her fingers gliding across his hand with its muck from the byre still on it. Yet nothing said, no acknowledgement made. Repeated glances towards the door, as if I might come in. Then growing boldness and the final grasping and coming together of flesh.

It was winter. The days lasted from nine till three, and all the rest was night. The house was surrounded by a sea of night, with that damned Orr forever paddling through it on his way here. He knew the welcome he would get.

It would be she who made the decisive moves, leaving him in no doubt. She would lay her hands on his, just as he was about to take another bite of scone, and look straight

at him. It's years since she looked straight at me. After that
the kissing would start. I could always tell when the kissing
had started because of the silences. Long mysterious gaps
in the constant murmur of talking and the chomp of scones.
It would be she, all right, that brought the flesh together.
She had always lusted after him, although I wasn't able to
see it before.

She would have started the rest of it too: the coupling,
like beasts in the fields. I would hear the door scraping as
they crept out to the barn. He would take his boots from
where they were warming by the Rayburn and go and warm
the rest of him on her. She would lead him by the hand
through the muck and the puddles, eager to get at it. I'll
never know how I didn't see it all before. A horseblanket
on a stinking pile of straw, she spreading her pale limbs in
the dark; the hurried dreadful thrusting; then back to the
kitchen. Sometimes I even heard her laughing at me. She'd
be saying how I was always useless anyway, even when my
legs and my loins were working.

A time came when they didn't even bother to go outside.
They just slipped the bolt over the door and did it right there
on the floor like brute beasts. They'd have done it here in
this bed, if I wasn't always in it.

Night's the worst. A whole year of nights lying watching
darkness lapping at the window, listening for sounds to
identify, hearing nothing. She in the room next door,
because she can't bear to sleep in a bed occupied
permanently by an invalid. It's become my world, this soft
rectangle. She says it smells like a den. Her slow breath in
the dark. Quickening occasionally when she dreams about
that damned Orr.

Autumn; wearing on towards winter. Trees like witches'
brooms, leafless, lifeless. Darkness dropping from a
bulging sky, and a passing threat of snow. The stark beasts
in the fields chomping at the poor grass like damned Orr at
the scones. The grass turning black in the distance as day
fails. A pale sound of mourning in the afternoons: geese
drift south erratically. It reaches me lying on my back in this
trap of a bed, the light failing all around me. I have wept to

hear that lonely creaking pass.

Then I began to do press-ups. I needed to strengthen my arms, so that I'd be ready when the time came. I wasn't going to let that damned Orr away with it.

The time came. I heard the clatter of his damned boots outside in the yard. He stepped in to see me, to salve his guilt, I suppose. I've not been up for a while he says. A lie like that should choke a man. He's been up all right. I never spoke a word to him, just stared at the window. The sky was fading from dark grey to black. I could see a moon, just a white glow behind the shifting clouds. After a while he left.

I heard the kitchen door shutting, then the clink of a teaspoon spinning tea in a cup. A murmur of voices. I could just picture his damned great jaws working through the scones, grinding away sideways as he watched her move around the kitchen. His eyes would never be off her. She would bathe in his look like a person lying in the sun, turning this way and that, showing one part of her body and then another. Finally the silence came, and I knew they were at their coupling. I heard the click of the bolt on the outside door. I lowered myself on to the floor with my arms, and managed to drag my legs out after me. The pressups had given me me the strength I needed.

Painfully I dragged myself across the floor, out the door, and down the hall. I had to stop halfway along the hall, and lie flat on my stomach for a while before carrying on, dragging myself like a creature out of a swamp.

At the kitchen door I stopped again. Not a sound came from inside. I listened for panting breath, the creak of a spring, her fluttering cries. Nothing. They were probably doing it on the floor. I got myself as close as I could to the door, reached up to the handle, and turned it. The door opened, swinging slowly away from me. My heart was racing like an engine with too much choke on. The kitchen was revealed to me foot by foot in the slow sweep of the door.

And there they were. He was sitting at the table with a magnifying glass strapped to his eye, and she was knitting. He was mending the damned kitchen clock, and the bits were all over the table. She went pale and stood up, and he opened his eyes so wide the glass fell out. They helped me back to bed, that damned Orr with his arm under my oxter. He's like a damned bullock. I just had to say I had felt like some exercise.

I told her the next day that I'd really been hoping to catch them at their illicit coupling, that I knew they'd been at for months, ever since I was withered in the accident. She held me in the dark fire of her eyes, a steady wordless denial, until I had to look down. I thought she wasn't going to speak, but she did. What could I think of her, she said, to think that. I felt ashamed. She had no interest whatever in that damned Orr, beyond simply neighbourly friendship. He had been working on the grandfather clock, and now the old school clock in the kitchen. She would knit, she said, while he fiddled away with the tiny parts of the clock, in silence. I believed her. It was so simple, she so sincere. She looked straight at me all the time she was speaking, a thing she hasn't done in years. I smiled. It was a relief. I drank some cocoa, then she helped me on to the commode. I felt embarrassed by the smell, but she was brisk and practical and opened a window. The night air was damp, and laden with the fetid smell of wild fungus. I lay in bed that night with the window still slightly open, for the first time in a year. The slow air drifted in, a torment and a joy to me.

Why I ever imagined she saw anything in that brute Orr, I have no idea. He's not half the man I was. We can share a joke now, she and I, that I know there was nothing in it. I told her the other night that she was putting on the beef as well as me, and she so skinny before; she didn't have my excuse. It must be all those scones you've been eating, I said to her, with that damned Orr. And she turned to me, and smiled strangely; just the slightest bending of the lips.

Meek (A Life)
Christopher Low

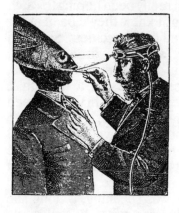

As he neared the top of the escalator Meek saw a U, presumably a reference to himself. At the bottom they hauled Meek clear, and his eyes focussed.

"Hi."

It was a girl.

"Hello," Meek said.

"I'm Miranda," the girl said. Her eyes twinkled in the lights. "Would you like to come with me?"

"Very much," replied Meek, who thought Miranda pretty.

"It's what I want," she said, "down there." Her eyes glistened.

Meek gasped. "You mean...?"

"The Outer Circle," said Miranda, and she smiled, and held out her hand.

Miranda's hand was even softer and gentler than Meek

had hoped. He allowed himself to be led to another escalator and from its end the couple stepped into a Great Hall.

Here Meek was dazzled by strip lights and shiny tiles and there was a trough in the middle of the floor linking twin holes at each end. As Meek talked to Miranda and found her nice as well as pretty he heard an ominous noise, and soon a train poked from one of the holes and braked in front of them. Although Meek felt uneasy he boarded the train with Miranda.

Sitting down on an orange checked seat, Meek heard a noise like a huge tyre deflating and the doors shut with a thump. Now Meek and Miranda were alone as the train murmured into one of the holes. It was then something nice happened. Afterwards Meek sat up, rubbed his eyes and as the train sighed to a stop yawned and peered from the window. He saw the words *Bridge Street.* Meek began to drum his fingers on his thigh as he waited for the train to restart. Soon it did.

The next time he saw *Bridge Street* the roar of the train had begun to irritate Meek. Miranda was no longer pretty except in a rather washed-out way and, he saw only too clearly, had never really been a nice person. There were lots of people now and Miranda was very involved in Outer Circle life. Meek had begun to read the words in the Halls outside the train, finding some consolation there. Once an Inner Circle train, humming and ticking to itself, had blocked his view.

One day Meek's train groaned into the tunnel and through the window black walls rushed past. The train rattled violently. As it cried to a stop Meek read *Hillhead.* He sighed, walked to the door and left the train.

Later an Inner Circle train was snarling into the darkness. Sitting guiltily inside was Meek. Here others were shadowy and silent, and Meek watched them rock on the two long seats. The train shook and roared. To pass the time Meek had devised a game in which he guessed the word in the next Hall. I'm certain it'll be *Hillhead*, Meek thought, where I left Miranda. In fact the sign read *Kelvinbridge*, but next time he guessed correctly.

Lighting a cigarette, Meek stared at *Hillhead*. There was a tap on his knee.

Meek turned. An old man sat to his right.

"Sorry?" said Meek.

"No smokin'," said the old man. "There's notices. Mind, I'm saying nothing." He sat back and folded his arms.

This was correct because on each end of the train red circles enclosed scored-out black cigarettes, and between the ridges in the wooden floor Meek couldn't see any cigarette ends.

"You would think," the old man said, "that owin' to the circumstances pertainin' to this particular journey they wouldny object to you having a wee smoke. Eh?"

Meek drew hard on the cigarette, threw it down and crushed it beneath his shoe.

"This journey?" he asked.

The old man looked at him. "Aye," he said.

He took a bottle from his pocket and after unscrewing the top and rubbing the neck hard offered it to Meek. The name on the bottle stirred a feeling of longing in Meek, for a golden land. He shook his head.

"No?" said the old man. He drank from the bottle and replaced it in his pocket.

"Later, possibly," Meek said. "And the others?" He glanced along the length of the coach where silent figures swayed.

"No not them," said the old man. "Not this time."

The train whined to a stop at the word *Kelvinhall*. Two young men with untidy bundles of books stood up and, when the doors parted, laughingly left the train. The doors slammed shut.

"I'll be alone," Meek said.

"No ways," said the old man.

"But..."

"There's me as well," said the old man. "It's just going to be the two of us."

"I see," said Meek. He turned and smiled at the old man.

"You've gone for the Inner one to finish up with," the old man said. "Not a bad choice. You're lucky to have been able to make that decision!"

"Mine have been very few," said Meek. "Decisions I mean. I seem to have gone round in Circles."

The old man looked at him sternly. "See me, I've had some bevvies, mainly in the Outer Circle if you understand my meaning. But I'm still fond of a bit of company even in this Inner one. Know what I mean?"

"Yes," said Meek, "and I've been happy to talk to you."

There was a noise like a siren dying and soon they were under the word *Partick*. No-one boarded. Then the doors closed and the train ground into the tunnel.

Black walls dashed past Meek's eyes and when he swallowed his ears cleared. Here it's very deep, he thought, as the train roared, perhaps under a great river. But at the word *Govan* the train shivered and stopped.

The doors scratched open and two figures rose and left hurriedly. Now only Meek remained with the old man. Alongside was an Outer Circle train and Meek could see what appeared to be a party. He heard faint raucous voices and clinking glasses and a woman laughing. With a dull shock Meek realised the woman was Miranda.

She leant towards an Outer Circle man and, when Meek waved, did not appear to recognize him, though she waved back politely.

"They're just enjoying theirsel's," the old man said. He drew the bottle from his pocket. "Can I no' tempt you?"

Meek nodded and took the bottle. His lips were dry. He drank the sticky liquid and returned the bottle. His hand trembled.

"Did you notice?" continued the old man by way of conversation, "that after the word *Govan* there's a break in the Circles? A tunnel branching off to the right?"

"Yes," said Meek. He shuddered, fumbled in his pocket and brought out a cigarette. He lit it.

"Have your smoke if you want to now son," the old man said.

The train whistled and hummed. When the cigarette was short Meek dropped it and twisted it under his shoe. It lay between the ridges of the wooden floor.
"I used to collect them," said the old man.
Then the doors hissed, and fused.

Meek closed his eyes as the train wailed into the void. And there the roar of the train stopped, and there was just the rattle of the wheels, and when Meek opened his eyes he saw in strip light the brick walls of a spacious cavern. Then the train lurched to the right.
Meek watched blackness streak past until, as if inevitably, the train lights went out.

A hand, rough like the branch of a tree, slid into Meek's.
"I wonder if there's a Great Hall at the end of all this," said Meek.
The old man did not reply and Meek, as he sat in the darkness, thought carefully about why this should be.

On The East Parade
Valerie Thornton

He'd been gone for thirteen nights. It was the longest they'd ever been apart. Each evening she had continued knitting his jersey of Shetland greys, with the brief single stripes of red, the colour of roses he'd given her. They had withered and died awhile since, but they remained on the kitchen table, dark, dried and distorted, in a dusty jam-jar from which the water had evaporated.

Each night she left the hall light on, and the storm door unlatched, so that when he returned to her he would feel welcomed. It was only when they were together, inside, that they shut out the rest of the world with chains and bolts.

She had even replaced his favourite ginger-bread, twice, so that he would have a fresh one when he returned.

She had waited in long enough for him. Now she was going to go out and look for him, to find him and assure herself that he was safe and well, wherever he was.

She would go first to where they had met, so many years ago. Not that she really expected him to be there, but it was a start. Apart from anything else, she was onto the last sleeve, and she knew he was looking forward to wearing it.

The terrace of houses with its gardens and trees, wasn't so very different. Although the cars had changed and the stone had been sandblasted to pale yellow, the puddled pot-holes on the roadway remained.

She wandered along calmly, feeling familiar, yet strange. She had walked here often, yet she'd been a different person then - young, and feeling love sharply in the heart. By now the feeling had suffused into an underlying current of loving and being loved.

The evening sun was striking through the autumn trees, mottling the upper half of the buildings with a shifting pattern of purples and ochre. There had been the same shifting pattern in his room when she had stayed overnight with him. In those heady days of sleepless nights they'd lain at peace in each others arms and watched the cold white streetlight shining through the branches, shifting and shivering on the dusty window. It would have been frightening without him.

A door opened ahead of her and a young man danced lightly down the steps to the pavement. For an instant her heart stopped - the young man was wearing a flying jacket like the one he had worn in those days. Once it had been raining and his jacket had been stained dark. She remembered too his fingernails - not black-grimed like a car mechanic's, but multicoloured with blue and yellow paint beneath the nails. But this man was too small, and too light of foot to be hers. He was moving quickly away from her, oblivious.

She came to their flats - she'd been renting the damp, spidery basement and he'd lived on the first floor.

They wouldn't have met but that she'd inadvertently turned off his water when she'd discovered a scalding overflow pipe spouting down like an inverted geyser at her back doorstep.

Well he certainly wasn't in the basement - she could see a white-haired old woman moving slowly behind the net curtains in that static environment of armchairs and ornaments which old people create around themselves. He had been there once - omelette plate balanced on the arm of the couch, mug of coffee at his elbow - but certainly not now.

She went up the steps to the main door. She ached to see the square of cardboard stuck to the green doorpost with four squares of yellow insulating tape, bearing his name. His stylised elongation of the letters had been so similar to her own that she'd accused him of copying her - but he'd merely smiled knowingly and pointed out that he'd been living there for two months longer than she had.

She quietly cursed the same old tartan and plastic *McDonald* for having a new brown Dymo-taped name below it, instead of his. There was obviously no point in ringing; he'd left there a long time ago.

She returned home, somewhat disheartened. She'd need to look in the right place. Where could he have gone to? Where had they been happy?

She decided to go to Wales. They had spent a few happy days there this summer. He must be far from home or he would have returned before now. She had finished his jumper anyway. It only needed sewn up and the rib at the neck knitted. That could wait until she returned.

She locked the windows and double-locked the doors before setting off. She retraced their route down the east coast of England and along the coast of North Wales. She smiled as she remembered their despair at the cheap little towns with beautiful Welsh names, dominated by the kilns and cooling towers of heavy industry, the air foul with sulphur. Then their continuing misery as this gave way to chip-shop and caravan-site holiday villages with half-empty amusement arcades.

Finally, exhausted, they arrived in Llandudno, a haven of quaintly decorative peace and quietness. Here, on the

East Parade, they had been amused by the rows of tourists sitting on deckchairs on the beach with the sea humbly lapping behind them, conceding the greater attraction of the sun, high in the south-west.

At night the long pier was iced with lights, stretching insubstantially out to sea past the headland. They had walked together along its boards, past shut souvenir kiosks, towards the music which drew them to the very end. There they had looked over the white railings to the dull metallic water below. They were standing in the bluish shadows beside an open-air dance floor where they could see the middle-aged couples dancing cheek to cheek in perfect harmony. These complicated dances were steps they had never learned; these old tunes were melodies they had never lived with. Yet they had found their hearts torn by nostalgia for something they had never known, and she had tears in her eyes.

He must be here. She left him here on the Victorian promenade one night. She'd been to a subterranean ladies' toilet lit only by the streetlights filtering through the thick green glass tiles in the roof. He was going on slowly.

When she climbed out, she glanced back before following him - and then she saw him. Enough of him to be him, sitting on a bench, leaning forward, long hands clasped, looking out to the dark sea. He had the same hair, the same silhouette in that light, yet she knew if she went to him the spell would break.

She left him waiting there and hurried after the familiar figure walking slowly ahead of her. He recognised her footsteps and turned, arm out to enfold her, a welcoming smile on his face.

Now she waited till evening. She wandered along the pier in daylight. The kiosks were open, but the old time dancing was shut and silent. The enchantment would return at night, she was sure of it.

She found the little restaurant they'd eaten in, and idly glanced inside to see if he was waiting there.

Then she wandered past the Alhambra Palace Theatre where she'd found a beautiful green-fired opal ring at an

Antiques Fair. The theatre was closed, but boasted future attractions in the form of films and pop concerts.

Evening came quickly now it was so late in the season. She pulled her woollen jacket tightly around her to ward off the sea wind.

The promenade was much quieter now - no bands of religious singers, nor aircraft displays - but he had to be here.

She walked for what seemed like hours, forcing herself to be calm, although inside she felt as tight as if a jack were in his box waiting to leap out and tear her heart to pieces.

She'd passed the bench where she'd left him. It was empty. The jack inside her prepared to jump.

Then she noticed, from the side of her willing yet unwilling eye, a half familiar form. With meticulous precision she forced herself to continue walking without faltering. She could not allow herself to indulge her gaze upon him. But she was certain it was him. The same graceful hands, composed stillness and curly hair - though his hair seemed to be a little longer.

No matter, it was enough of him to be him. She now had to pass him without attracting his attention. From her sidelong glances - all that she dared allow herself - she was certain that he hadn't noticed her. Nor must he - it would shatter the spell.

She lost him from her vision and counted a further two hundred steps before allowing herself to cross the broad promenade and sit down on a bench. She was shivering violently. It had been him - there must be no doubt - within earshot, sight and reach. She could have sat beside him, had she chosen to, buried her face in his neck and inhaled the soft animal scent of him. But he had left her - he had obviously wanted to be alone - and he must want to come back to her.

Carefully, she turned her head to look back along the rows of benches curving away from her. He had gone. She should have known. His place was empty. Someone was walking away, far in the distance - a shadow which might or might not be him.

She returned home reassured, and completed his jumper. Of course they had been wrong. She was now certain of that. Why did they talk about some kind of accident when he'd only gone back to Llandudno? It was some kind of conspiracy against her. He'd be back soon. Even her brother was trying to confuse her, going on about identifying some body because she'd been too upset or something.

What nonsense! She knew where he was. He would be back soon.

That night, after she closed the unlocked storm doors, she laid out his new jersey so that it would be the first thing he saw when he came back to her.

Already she could see the smile on his face.

Berlin
Alex Benzie

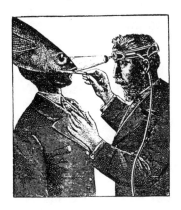

T here's a bar in the city centre where ethereal creatures make conversation, drink sweet frothy cocktails, indulge in easy desperate pairings. Its front is a benediction of rainbow neon and mirrored glass, lambent by night, with queues of sharp dressers waiting to get into the basement. Once there, you're served at a slab of sky blue marble; glasses slim and elegant as vases spill the occasional bubble ring, quickly wiped away. You might even be invited to join a group to be analysed, pinned there by wit, atomically scrutinised before being discarded. If you're there with friends, you're probably regulars. You will drink light frisky spirits shaded under paper parasols, in diamond glasses clinking with bullets of ice and a cartwheel of lemon; you will smoke cigarettes slender as pencils, exhale it in a bright surrounding nimbus. Your conversation will drift and wander with the group, and you will laugh often. Your music will come crisp and treble-clean from meshed boxes on the wall; unobstructive but enough to alleviate the occasional dread fall into the abyss of silence.

Above all, you must never, ever be serious. What are you anyway, some kind of neurotic?

The decor? Cold tinted mirrored shiny; what the easily pleased, the uncritical, might call sophisticated. You as a regular know why you're here. It's quintessentially tacky. Christ, you could bite the glassy pillars and find them made of some fragile, deliquescent confection. Character? No, darling. Tat. But the purest. You've got everything you need here to keep you warm, to blunt the edge of the chilling boredom.

You must find the ceramic wall over there in the far corner intriguing; after all, the casual, visiting drinkers do. Oh, you must've noticed it; the arms reaching out to you from the smooth ice. A sculpture? Not exactly, nor is it really a mural. What it is; as if the wall is an ocean placed on edge, so the careless swimmers are clawing the water's skin, looking for help from the shore, finding none, just curiosity. A face, strong jawed but sexless. The floating arc of a female torso. The face is resigned and perhaps amused; could belong to any of the limbs.

Tacky. Delicious. The name of the bar, ladies and gentlemen, is Berlin.

The material is ideal, the form is ideal; it'd be a pity to waste it.

Let's watch as the after-hours darkness thickens and gathers together its folds, tighter and tighter until something's got to give, nothing can be that compact. There, the release; a scream of birth trauma as the swimmers push against their prison into the vacuum of identity, stone-made-flesh brittle and elastic all at once, forming around granite bone. A compromise is struck, allowing them existence in the shape of two men, one woman. The gift is apparently grudged, however; they're still reined to the wall by white strands, not quite skin, not quite ceramic, finally thinning like tendrils of molten pizza cheese, snapping, healing, becoming calm again. They sprawl exhausted on the couches, naked as the day they were born; which this is, if you think about it. As an afterthought they are granted a neat ziggurat of folded clothes. They don't have names, so we might as well call them Marcus, Paulus and Claudia. Do they look too perfect to you? Perhaps they need to be, if they're to be made so completely welcome here.

Marcus is the first to breathe, raising his new hand, staring freshly at its cords and mounts.

--Gawd, I'm so stiff. (Paulus's eyes widen, framed by arch, arched eyebrows.) Oh, witty. Wit-tee.

--Then don't tell lies, dear. I can see you're not.

Claudia stands finally on unfamiliar legs, tautly muscled; stretches to shake the imprisoned tension out of her, relaxes at the crescendo.

--Good to be out again. I'd forgotten what it was like to have a blood supply.

Paulus massages something uncomfortable in the globe of his calf, gasping as it unfolds.

--Ow. I hope we don't have to go back. Cramps a fellow's . . . ow.

--Hypochondriac, sniffs Claudia. Now that she's satisfied with her golden appearance, she peels clothing from the pile and shrugs into them; dressed, you can see she is immaculately designed, showing off a high heeled walk as fluent and threatening as the stalking of a panther. She begins to apply make up, flashing a hand through spiky dark hair, using a panel of mirrors to guide the layers and contours.

--I think we may be more fortunate tonight, says Marcus, stepping into a dark cotton suit. It gives him the clean, ascetic look of the priest; or maybe the assassin, touching lives like a plough-share, moving on.

--Hopefully, says Claudia, turning to face him. Eye shadow glints cool and steely, like shutters, lips are glossed a preterhuman red.

--Bored already, love? Not the company, I trust, says Paulus, struggling into a loose drapery of trashy material which manages to arrange itself into a kind of vagrant elegance. He has quick, nervous sparrow's eyes which treat everything as threat, never fix on anything; when he deals syllables, they're played confidently for trumps.

--I think that's us, says Marcus.

--About time. It's been bloody ages, says Claudia, loudly and bitterly enough for an audience to hear, but there's only the wall.

--Who cares? It'll be fun, says Paulus. Get yourself a nice hunky man. That'll be nice, won't it dear?

--Perhaps. Why, you might even be that lucky.

She gives him a look as pure as innocence, drawing a smirk from him.

--God grant us all such good fortune, in a way, says Marcus dryly. Now let's go. It's beginning to disgust me, this place.

Our additive laden air seems sweet to them as they go on a night walk. Claudia strays to a nearby court building and lets her fingers wander along the dimples and canyons of sandstone. On a ledge stands Justice clasping the sword and scales, flanked by two impassive caryatids representing mercy and betrayal, almost corrosive. Marcus notices how morose she has become, how her glitter has dulled.

--D'you want to stay here? (She shakes her head.) Come on. Let's go somewhere else.

The docks are desolate, but the sodium light ornaments the dull river. Their footsteps panic a tabby cat plump with kittens, sniffing the tangy air, shifting away from the nest she chose mostly by instinct; scoots up a metal gangway into the safety of darkness.

--No one here, says Paulus. Christ.

--What's wrong with you? says Claudia.

--What's the bloody smell?

--Old machine oil, stuff spilled from cargo ships, explains Marcus. No one works here any more. It's all been left to rot.

--I'm not surprised, says Paulus, calling, Hello!

--Wh'sat? says someone from a monolith of shadow, voice heavy with phlegm. An old man rises to his feet, shuffles over to them and into the light, a crackling shell of gabardine from which he peers out, a sad invertebrate creature looking for its bones, crusted with barnacles of filth. He looks them over with milky eyes. Paulus recoils from the animal smell creeping around the flaps of the old man's coat.

--Don't worry, says Marcus. We're only visiting.

--Sat right? Come here f'r a good laugh?

--Not really. Healthy curiosity. No other reason.

-- Fucking tourist. I have to live here. (His rheumy eyes look across the waterfront.) Used t'work here. Whasup, nose bothering you?

Paulus defends his delicate nostrils with the back of his hand.

--In a manner of speaking.

--Bastard. Well t'hell with you. Go on, have a look around. No bugger else wants it.

The shards of his teeth, the chips which aren't eroded, gleam in the sodium light; and the breath which so offends Paulus is foul with cheap fortified wine and thrown up takeaways, glistening carelessly on the coat.

--I'm touched. (Paulus notices a wrapped bottle in the man's hand, snatches it from him with a swift chameleon's lick.)

What's this?

--Don't, whimpers the man, gimme ....

Paulus peels back the paper, furled around the bottle like the collar of a lily, sniffs the mouth cautiously. He takes a brief pull as an experiment, spits it out explosively; by all rights it should ignite on the ground. Marcus smiles.

--An auspicious vintage.

Paulus draws his hand across the fire on his lips.

--My fucking teeth're melting.

--Gimme it back, mister. Please.

Paulus pinches the bottle's neck between thumb and forefinger, holds it out like a soiled rag.

--Is this all you've got?

It makes a crazy sound on the cobbles, a beggar's glissando, and the man falls to his knees, shapeless as he begins to sob; dropping and pulling his tongue along the ground.

--That was cruel, says Claudia, who quite enjoyed the little drama really.

--Crap, says Paulus as they step through a gap in the gate. It was for his own good.

--How lucky we are, muses Marcus, when we can consider our evils as perverse acts of kindness.

--Fuck off, says Paulus. He deserved it.

Chandlers' squats between a disused warehouse and a very fashionable hair salon, casting fibres of lurid light on the river like scribbles on a black-board; you might recognise some of the people here from earlier on. From inside you can probably make out a series of detonations, the pulsing and hammering of a hyperactive heart worked almost to bursting. The three buy drinks and sit on couches placed in friendly shade, away from prying sweeps of spot glare, for the moment noting and sizing. Paulus laughs at the smoke hissing through the clenched teeth of a floor level grille; Marcus points to how the sequenced lights drip and swirl into it, like a child's paint brush discharging and dissolving into a jar of water. A bubble machine releases small planets to float and iridesce in the warm distorted air, some popping emptily, others pinballing among the tall crystal pillars as they shoot neon spirals into the curves of the vaulted ceiling. If they survive that, they stand a fair chance of blundering into the cat's cradle of green lasers scrawling stars on the walls, on the dancers.

Marcus indulges a smile, sips his nectarous drink.

--So this is what I came here for, he says, too softly to be heard.

Paulus notices the motion of his mouth.

--We can't sit here all night, he calls into Marcus's ear. We've got to try.

--Patience, says Marcus. I know.

It's all so easy. Marcus and Paulus stalk the floor, and the market yields up its goods; two demure doe eyed young things shiny with blusher and body frost. Paulus regrets the ease of it all, since he had been rather looking forward to a man tonight. Oh well, they move nicely anyway, and their shyness melts gradually, a sugar strategy to interest you in the satisfying dessert of personality, daring more. Sheila glances at Marcus from under a full canopy of teased blonde hair, flirting wickedly. Sandi (with an *i*, she clarifies) says Paulus looks smart. He thanks her with a fatuous smile, all she deserves, really.

Claudia has attracted a gaudily dressed wasp of a man who leans over her with total confidence, protecting her with his shadow. She does him the reciprocal service of looking interested in what he's got to say; lets him lead her to the floor. She catches Paulus's jealous looks, caresses Adam's cheek with red almond fingertips.

In Berlin, switches are thrown, light crashes down from the ceiling, without mercy; Marcus softens it, giving it the texture of melted butter. Sandi gazes around.

--Hey, it's really nice. You must be proud of it. Must've set you back a bit, too.

Marcus and Paulus share ironies with each other, a glance and nothing more.

--Would you like a drink? says Marcus.

Sheila looks out from under her fringe and tisks severely.

Marcus puts a kiss on his fingertips and touches it to her lips; she receives it generously, then asks for creme de menthe. Sandi asks for something with a mysterious, French-sounding name. Paulus slots a tape into the machine behind the bar, presses the play tab. Slow, creamy music spills from the speakers, and the girls move idly to the rhythm, weaving back to their seats. Claudia arrives, her waist in the cradle of Adam's arm.

--At bloody last, dear, says Paulus. Where have you been?

--Just dallying. This is Adam, by the way.

--Is it? says Marcus. Would Adam like a drink?

--God, yeah, could murder a whisky. Glenlivet, if you've got one. (To Claudia;) I don't think you said...

--Don't worry about it. Just call us inseparable.

The girls giggle, now a bit drunk. A few more, and they become malleable, ready for shaping. Marcus dims the lights to a simple glaze; takes Sheila by the hand to the seclusion of a corner couch, lies there with her.

--Forever? she says.

--Until morning, he says, undressing her.

Outside the sun peers over the rim of the horizon.

Marcus, Paulus and Claudia stir their partners. Come on, I want to show you something. They gather in the far corner, guarding their nakedness and trying not to make it look like overly fussy modesty.

--What is it? says Sandi. What have you got to show us?

It isn't that dramatic really, as if the world tilted sideways and a force like gravity drew them into a white pond; the girls scream, and Adam claws the white meniscus for help, finding none, just curiosity. Sandi presses her face out while the stone still thinks it's flesh, but the ceramic layer closes over them after its rupture, crystallising over their petrified bodies; chilling them with what it knows, how trapped, how alone they are.

Hear anything? It's so quiet you can almost hear the betrayal settling like dust.

They dress rapidly. Before going upstairs, Claudia turns back.

--Your turn next, she says, with a little pity, if no real guilt.

The door opens for them. All the remembered smells are there, sweet and sharp and chemical. Now true flesh, they wait for night.

Sharp Practice
Lorn Macintyre

M r. Manson descended into the subway breeze, that smell unique to Glasgow; Stockholm tar used on the construction, or so they said. He kept his umbrella close to his leg, like a ceremonial sword.

They went risking their ankles down the steps in the rush-hour, but he knew that a train wouldn't come rumbling before he reached his platform; the telegraphy of long experience, as if he could feel the tremor of it leaving the next station up the loop. The wall was always within reach.

He left his office at five fifteen precisely, by his father's pocket watch. (You couldn't trust those digital things with their black faces. Time should tick away close to you, to be weighed in the hand; no better signal for a meeting at an end.)

He was the senior partner. He could have retired two years' past, having paid into a sound pension fund. He certainly didn't need to turn out each day for the money. He'd been lucky, getting a full quota of British Telecom shares.

In his younger days he'd liked the thrust of court work; the opponent's guard dropped, the *coup de grace* that convinced the sheriff. Now he confined himself to checking conveyancing deeds. Mistakes were made; arguments over an inch of boundary fence could lead to violence.

The young men (and women; far too many) being turned out by the law faculties nowadays were brash, ambitious, wanting partnerships before they had any real experience. But then, hadn't so many other things changed for the worse?

Home was in Hillhead; a leafy place in the city, a suburb in itself when he'd started out nearly 50 years before. They had the whole house, but there had never been any question of letting the top to students.

Mildred and he had no children; not that there had been much opportunity. Still, it was a settled existence; already he was turning the corner, the residents' parking round the railed gardens which no dogs were allowed to foul.

He was giving two twists to the mortice lock as well as the Yale. You couldn't be too careful; two houses within shouting distance had been done, and Mildred had a valuable collection of Scottish watercolours inherited from an uncle. Insurance wasn't replacement.

The cat (their third; the last one dozing under a delivery van) wound round his leg in the hall; that aroma of beeswax; none of your rubbish spray polishes that evaporated as soon as they struck wood, Mildred said. And no home help either, come to that.

He put his hat on the same hook, his umbrella below. He doesn't need to go through to the kitchen; she's heard the door. He goes up the brass-rodded staircase to the drawing-room, reflective with inherited surfaces on both sides. He tilts his pale sherry from faceted glass before going to sit under the floral hood of the standard lamp.

He sips, relaxing before dinner (He's already read the *Herald* over his solitary frugal lunch at a restaurant table that has become his own). He may put on a record, one from his collection in their original envelopes with cellophane portholes; not a scratch, the static trawled religiously by a black velvet pad, the needle changed every six months by the local electrician. He plays them on a thirty year old British machine with folding walnut doors he wouldn't dream of changing.

Rachmaninov is a mountain stream to this once-keen hillwalker, trim nape on his mother's needlework till Mildred beats brass with the padded stick.

The rubber-lipped doors of the subway car divided at his shoes. He didn't step aside; those coming off had to go round the elderly man. He took the seat nearest the exit, umbrella between his knees, briefcase (the buckled kind) laid on his knees.

Someone sat beside him. As the train went into darkness the thought was travelling with him again, the season ticket of age; on a branch line, himself, alone, rocked gently toward Elysian Fields, the terminus beyond the suburbs; a bright place, with flowers, his own plot.

With Mildred? Ah, there's the question. If you've spent your life with one person (she'd been a childhood friend, the marriage as inevitable as his inheritance of his father's house) do you really want to spend eternity with her? Mildred did the walled garden, pressing in bulbs with her gauntlets, in her baggy mannish corduroys; and twice a year she waddled round the path with the nozzle, the opaque shell on her back.

Surely in Paradise, capitalised, you didn't have to fork over the loam, dribbling in bone-meal? And this dark Crombie coat cut in the old style would have to go, with the striped sleeves under it, down to the skin.

He rested his chin on crossed hands on the crozier of the umbrella. A girl in black sandshoes, her pantaloons bagged to the ankles was reading a holiday brochure. He was sailing down the coast with his parents; the beat of the paddle; blowy dresses.

Baby Of Anne's Dream the catchphrase in the tabloid

between a workman's fists.

Opposite him a woman sat with her tartan zipper bag on tyres down to the rims.

This Seat Is Intended
For The Elderly, The Disabled
And The Infirm

So far he qualified on one count. But he was definitely getting slower and couldn't hold the signature from the broad nib that had also served his father.

But the thought of being at home all day, confined, frightened him. He didn't want to depend on television; everything was violence, the news nothing but the rubble of Beirut where religions he didn't understand were battling it out. Two nights ago there had been a home-made video on the Ten bulletin; in the flickering frame a bearded American, fifteen months in captivity, begging the President, and all the time barrels sloped to each temple.

They had very few friends in a city they'd both been born in. You had to watch a fall; several neighbours had gone through fractured hips, the natural selection of slippery pavements. The swaying umbrella lurched him into more rumination; feet came, went, the shabby chariot of the shopping trolley pulled out backwards by the woman in the sponge bootees. Where was the saving when it had to be hoisted up steps into the night, and probably more to a high-rise home, the lift burnt out? Imagine not being able to get a coffin down. They should bring back hanging.

Clattered along under a city he'd left so seldom; to university there, not even a subway ride away. He hadn't dared to say he wanted to read English. On the day war had been declared, men had left the lecture theatre to enlist. He wanted the horizons of the navy but his father had wangled fire-watch duties after classes.

On the second night of the Clydebank blitz he'd found a charred baby under rafters he was hosing.

And for what? he mused as the doors shut out another

station. They had infilled the docks, levered up the tram-lines. The city had become a racetrack; safer to travel down here. But some things hadn't changed; the Botanic Gardens, where he and Mildred had held hands in the humidity of high glass.

There had once been a typist, raised on the most slender heels, the skirt slit beyond the knee. Dictation had been difficult. Each night he'd waited while she hooded the manual typewriter, but had never been able to ask her for a cup of tea. Once he'd gone to buy her nylons for Christmas, but had lost courage in the store's revolving door.

No; this was Thursday; Mildred was conveying the lamb casserole in her insulated mittens, her skull showing through her wispy hair. She was always busy, and even when they were watching TV (they were very selective) it was as if she was pulling the wool out of her own side in the wing arm-chair as the needles crossed.

They were Baptists, but that wasn't the same either. As a boy going with his parents he remembered the elegant white robed women stepping in for immersion. One girl, a student who was obviously doing the rounds of the religions, had come in a shiny bathing suit. The hem of the robe was weighted with leads. When she rose, dripping, baptised, her nipples protruded.

He collected art books, the human form by old masters. He liked to study them when he was alone. Titian's Venus Anadyomene stood in the sea, looking at something out of the picture, the rope of her hair held in both hands. A shell floated. The body was heavy, out of proportion, yet so - what was the word? But Mildred, glimpsed through an ajar door, gripping the chrome handles, hauling herself up in the steam. That hip needed attention.

The girl beside him jumped up.
"You touched me!"
His briefcase slid from his knees; the umbrella clattered across the aisle like a struck foil.
The youth with her had clawed off his headphones, was

punching his Walkman for silence.

"Touched me!"

"Dirty old bugger. I'll have you for this!" he said.

Clutching the post in both hands, Mr. Manson was confronted by washed-out denims. Then shoes, flimsy and stout, as passengers swayed round him. His homburg was knocked askew. Now the train was failing and he was being set upon in the darkness. The only mercy in death was immediacy; on the Attenborough series, the slow-motion dragging-down of the striped flank by the lion was surely misrepresenting nature; all over so much sooner.

The youth had him by the lapels, was lifting him face to face as if about to head-butt, the girl's face at his shoulder.

He was hauled off at the next stop, briefcase kicked after him, but the umbrella going on. It had his father's initials on the gold collar.

"You go for the polis!" he told his girlfriend.

Two trains came in different directions. Mr. Manson tried to turn and hide his face in case there were business acquaintances on their way home; but that only put his arm further up his back.

A man in soiled sheepskin came.

"What are you doing to him?" he demanded.

"It's a mugging," the victim whimpered. "I have trouble with my heart."

"Mugging fuck all," the youth said. "You feel in his pocket and you'll find his wallet. This is a pervert." He tightened the arm. "He touched my girlfriend on the train."

The suede shoulders shrugged and went on their way. Mr. Manson turned his head to the sunken lane of the track. If there really was a live rail down there, how come that rats could run? But that wasn't the way out.

The accuser was coming back with a policeman.

"It's a mistake," Mr. Manson pleaded.

"We'd better all go to the station," he told them, taking the youth's arm from Mr. Manson's.

He went up the steps first, but the wall seemed too far away. He remembered the trailer of the kind of television programme he would never watch: the man turning, lashing out with his attache case. But these legs wouldn't take him up and away.

"I've someone waiting at home," he said, panting, a hand inside his coat.

"I'd forget that," the youth advised. "You're for the jail, Mister."

The lights of Glasgow through the venetian slats were a rippling tide up to his chest. The detective constable across the mock teak was reading.

"I did not touch her."

"*Not* underlined," the accused advised him.

"Occupation?"

Mr. Manson had a choice of words here. He considered, clasped hands under his chin, waiting till he had the attention of the opposite face.

"I am a solicitor."

Was he taking it as a joke?

But the face had straightened again. "Then you'll know the procedure," the detective said.

"Am I being charged?"

He didn't answer that one. Instead he pressed a button on his phone.

"I need your address," the detective told him.

He had the biro poised, but Mr. Manson felt in his coat and put his nose into the folded handkerchief.

"This room is cold," he complained.

The door opened; another detective put a paper in front of his colleague and withdrew without a word. Mr. Manson needed his spectacles to read, far less upside down.

"This is the young woman's statement," the detective said. "I have to warn you that anything -"

Mildred would have the fireproof casserole on the front burner; a blistering stew of bay-leaves. She's gone through to the hall; no hat, no umbrella, the cat sitting, tail coiled, eyes large, alert, watching for a shadow beyond art nouveau glass. Her first thought (hands at her lined face): Oh my God a coronary; dying gasping as the subway rocked him home; maybe going the whole circuit before anyone realised that the old man in the corner wasn't sleeping.

Now he would really know what like it was to stand in that box, the sheriff's friendship of no help. You couldn't keep that sort of thing out of the papers. He would have to resign his partnership; probably both of them from the church.

Mr. Manson reached over. He took back his statement and tore it in half. "Give me another one."

He uncapped his father's nib. Sometimes he paused, wanting a word, a phrase. He didn't like scoring out. Opposite him a thumb was getting impatient with a throwaway lighter. At Kelvinside Academy the Manson English compositions were read out to the others, but when he took them home to his father, no comment. In his signature the letters were well rounded, the loops made.

"Have you blotting paper?"

The detective shook his head, so Mr. Manson gave it thirty seconds before passing it across. The detective's face was changing as he went through it, a finger rapidly tapping off ash.

"Read it out to me," the writer requested.

"I boarded the train at St Enoch's at 5.18pm., a habit for more years than I care to recall. As always I took the seat nearest the doors; not that that is an advantage in the event of a failure *en route.* My briefcase was laid across my knees, my umbrella standing between them. There is not the space in these new carriages, though the livery is brighter. (How does the upholstery escape the vandal's blade?)

Remember that this is a rush-hour train. At Cowcaddens a young woman came on with the crowd (It used to be even busier, but the city has suffered so many job losses). She was wearing denim which will not stretch any further, and which must do damage to young women. Her hair was long, dark; a mare's tail touching the back of my hand. As the train entered the tunnel I moved the hand from my briefcase and placed it on her thigh. How can this be done when there are people sitting opposite, their knees almost touching mine? By sliding the briefcase across with my other hand.

I took my hand away for St George's Cross, where there is always an exit because of the large ethnic community. As we pulled out of this station my hand was between her thighs. They were substantial.

The train rocks on this stretch of the line; perhaps they got their levels wrong when they were renovating it. The opposite windows become mirrors; she was smiling as we rocked together. Then her thighs started to tighten on my hand, though I wear my father's signet ring with an engraved black stone.

I was not aware that the young man with his cropped head clamped in earphones was with her. He must have come to the end of the tape strapped to his chest and noticed my hand. What else could she do but jump up and accuse me?"

The detective was screwing out his low-tar filter while watching him. Then he buzzed the phone, picked up both statements and went out. One of Mr. Manson's legs was sleeping. He got up and went to the window, parting the slats with two fingers. The rush hour was over. Then he moved his face closer to the map on the wall.

Buildings were rubbish nowadays; the timber frames would collapse before there was dust on the title-deeds. The muffled voices, one a woman's, were rising. There was Hillhead; his crescent. A man was shouting now, the racket let out into the corridor. The woman's Glasgow accent got shriller, her boyfriend swearing, the detective placating; then a slap.

Mr. Manson turned his head slowly, to see the pieces of paper tossed up into the small square of wire glass.

Heels clattered; doors came back.

"This is a nice map of Glasgow," Mr. Manson said, folding his spectacles into their steel case which you couldn't buy nowadays.

"That's one of the cleverest moves ..."

"I must caution you; I'm a solicitor."

D

"Get out," the detective said, tossing the torn sheets into the wastepaper basket.

"No, not like that," Mr Manson said, sitting again. "It was your lot who dragged me in here for nothing. I have a wife waiting whom I wish to phone. Then you will take me home."

"We don't run a taxi service."

"You will take me home in an unmarked car, otherwise..."

The officer lifted across the phone. Mr. Manson hadn't used the push-button type before and had to be shown.

It hardly rang; a shrill voice.

"Mildred, I know how worried you are, but the subway broke down between stations and we've just been released. Yes, yes, take the casserole to the dining-room; I'll be home in fifteen minutes."

My Happiest Day
Viktoria Tokareva

Translated by Stephen Mulrine

We were given a class essay to write on the subject of *The Happiest Day of My Life*. I spread out my notebook and tried to think - what was the happiest day of my life? I picked a Sunday, four months ago, when Papa and I went to the cinema in the morning, and drove out to Granny's straight after. A two-fold treat. But our teacher Marya Yefremovna says man is only genuinely happy when he is bringing some benefit to people. And how does that benefit people, that I was at the cinema, and then went out to Granny's? I could disregard Marya Yefremovna's opinion, but I need a decent mark for the term. I might even get a "Satisfactory" this term, and still not get promoted to the ninth grade. Marya Yefremovna has warned us that there's a surplus of intellectuals in the country now, and a shortage of workers, so they're going to create a pool of qualified workers, using us.

I sneaked a look at my neighbour's notebook, that's Lenka Konovalova. Lenka was scribbling away at an incredible rate, completely carried away. Her happiest day was the day she was accepted into the Pioneers.

I remembered the day we were all accepted into the

Pioneers, at the Border Guards Museum, and how they didn't have a Pioneer badge for me. The sponsors and troop leaders started running around, but they couldn't find one. "It's all right," I said, "It doesn't matter..." But it spoiled my mood, and after that I stopped paying attention. They took us round the museum, and told us its history, but I couldn't remember a thing.

I turned round to the right and looked over Mashka Gvozdeva's notebook. She sits in front of me. I wasn't able to make any of it out, but Mashka's probably writing that her happiest day was when the old particle accelerator in the lab blew up, and they had to give us a new one. That Mashka's just crazy about diagrams and formulas. She has outstanding mathematical ability, and she already knows where she's headed. She has a philosophy of life. The only thing I have is a good stock of words, which I can summon up at will. That's why I get the reports to do in the music class, on the life and works of the composers. The teacher writes a piece about the music, and I read it out from his notebook. For example: "Beethoven was a plebeian, without private means, and everything he achieved in life, he achieved by his own labours..." And I also make the announcements at concerts, for example: "Sonatina by Clementi, played by Katya Shubina, Mr. Rossolovsky's class". And it sounds convincing, because I have the height and colouring, and the right dress for the occasion. The colouring and the clothes have been handed down from Mama, but I don't know where I got the height from. I read somewhere that these modern panel-construction buildings, that don't let the air circulate, create conditions similar to a greenhouse, and that's why children grow so tall, like cucumbers under glass.

Mashka Gvozdeva will undoubtedly fetch up in the intelligentsia, because her brains'll be of more benefit to people than her hands. But I've got neither hands nor brains - just a stack of words. It's not even literary talent - I just know a lot of words because I read a lot. I get that from Papa. Knowing a lot of words isn't all that useful, however.

The boys in our class get by comfortably on half a dozen: spot on, okey-doke, ace, no probs, triffic, at this moment in time. And Lenka Konovalova can keep up a conversation with two sentences - "Well, yes, generally speaking. . . " and "Well, of course, as a rule. . . " And that's perfectly adequate: in the first place, she gives the other person a chance to speak, and that's always appreciated; and secondly, she keeps them guessing. "Well, yes, generally speaking. . . " "Well, of course, as a rule. . . "

I heard a programme about happiness on the radio last week. They were saying that happiness is when you want something, and you're trying to achieve it. And the greatest happiness is when you want something very badly, and you're trying very hard to achieve it. So it's true, then, that when you do achieve it, happiness ends, because happiness is the road to fulfilment, but not fulfilment itself.

So what do I want very badly? I badly want to be promoted to the ninth grade, to get into the Arts Faculty at Moscow University, and to meet the actor VV. Mama says it's quite natural to fall in love with actors at my age, twenty years ago she too loved an actor to distraction, and their entire class was going mad about him. And now this actor's fat and gone to seed - you just wouldn't believe it, what time does to people.

But Mama doesn't understand me - I'm not at all in love with VV. It's just that he plays D'Artagnan, and plays him so amazingly well that it's as if VV actually was D'Artagnan himself, talented, unpredictable, romantic. Not like our boys: spot on, okey-doke, *and* an inch shorter than me.

Rita and I once waited for VV after the performance, and followed him; we got into the same metro compartment and sat watching him. Whenever he looked in our direction, we turned away and started giggling. Rita found out about him through friends, and she told me VV was married, with a little boy. I'm glad it's a son, and not a daughter, because they're fonder of daughters, and don't show as much affection to boys, which means a bit of his heart is left free for a new love.

Lenka Konovalova has turned over another page - she's filled up half a notebook already. And I'm still sitting, groping around in my memory for my happiest day.

Actually, if I'm honest about it, my happiest days are when I come home from school and there's nobody in. I like my mother. She doesn't give me a hard time, doesn't make me do my music, or eat bread with my soup. I can do exactly the same when she's there, as when she's not there. Even so, it's not all roses. For instance, she's terribly careless putting the needle down on a record and it makes an earsplitting crackle through the loudspeakers, as if the needle's scratching at my heart. I say to her, "Why can't you put it down properly?" and she says, "I am putting it down properly." It's the same every time.

When she's out, there's a note on the door. "Keys under mat. Dinner in oven. Home at six. Be good. Love, Mama."

I read in a newspaper that Moscow comes out bottom of the list for crime in the world. That is, Moscow is the most peaceful capital city in the world. And that's true. I've proved that from my own experience. If some really nasty burglar-type, or maybe even just some nosy person with criminal inclinations, say, were to come up our stairs and read Mama's note, they would get precise instructions: key under mat - open the door, it's all yours; dinner in the oven - heat it up and tuck in, the mistress of the house'll be home at six. So they don't need to hurry, they can even relax in the armchair with a newspaper, and then clear off around six, with Papa's jeans and leather jacket under their arm, and Mama's sheepskin coat. Mama says if a person's frightened of being robbed, then they definitely will be. Whatever people are afraid of in life, that's just what's going to happen. So you should never be afraid. And that's absolutely true. If I'm frightened I'm going to be asked about my homework, then I definitely will be asked.

Whenever I come out of the lift and see the note I'm delighted, because I can do what I like, without having to suit anybody else. I go into the house. I don't heat anything up, just eat it straight out of the pot, with my coat on still, and standing up. Cold food tastes better. It loses its flavour when it's heated.

Then I turn on the record player full blast and call up Lenka Konovalova to come over. We whip all Mama's dresses out of the wardrobe, try them on and start dancing around in them. We're dancing in long frocks, and the Bluebirds are wailing, *Don't blame me, baby, don't take it bad -- don't call me up, don't feel so sad -- don't keep knocking at love's door...* And the sun's streaming in the window.

Lenka leaves then, and I settle down in the armchair, wrapped up in a travel rug, and start to read. Right now, I'm reading two books: short stories by Julio Cortazar, and plays by Alexander Vampilov. I like the scene in Vampilov where he says: "Papa, we have a guest, and he's brought somebody else with him." And the father says, "Vasenka, if our guest has brought somebody else, that makes two guests..."

When I read that I can just see VV - and that makes me sad, because he's married anyway, and there's a big difference in our ages.

And in Cortazar's story *The End of the Game*, there's the phrase "inexpressibly wonderful". That has such an effect on me that I look up from the page and start thinking. Sometimes just being alive seems inexpressibly wonderful. But other times it all just gets to be a bore, and I ask Mama, "What do people live for?" And she says, "To suffer. Suffering's the rule."

And Papa says, "It's the rule for idiots. Man was created for happiness."

And Mama says, "You forgot to add - like birds for flight. And you're the one that says pity debases people."

Papa says, "Well, of course it does. That's because only fools and halfwits expect pity. A wise man counts on himself."

And Mama says pity means compassion, sharing another's suffering, which holds the world together, and that's a talent which not even many wise men can manage.

But they don't argue all that often, because they rarely see each other. When Papa's home in the evenings, Mama's out. And vice-versa. If Mama's out, Papa reads his paper and watches ice-hockey on television. (We used to have a babysitter who couldn't pronounce ice-hockey properly, and called it "sockey"). When he's finished watching the "sockey", and read his paper, Papa demands to see my homework diary and starts shouting at me as if I was deaf, or in the apartment next door, so he's trying to make himself heard through a wall. When Papa starts shouting, for some reason or other I'm not frightened, but I simply can't understand him. I'd really like to say, "Don't shout, please, just speak quietly." But I say nothing, just blink my eyes.

Sometimes Mama gets home quite late, but she's still in before him. She sees his sheepskin coat's not on its hook, and she's terribly pleased.

But whenever Mama has private study days, and she's at home the whole time, she cooks the dinner for a few day's ahead, and my father isn't in until late at night - that's when she'll appear in my room, couldn't care less that I want to sleep, and not to have a conversation, and that really gets on my nerves. And she'll say, "If you want my opinion, he's walked out on us." And I say, "So what about his leather jacket and jeans? He wouldn't go away without them."

"But he can come back for them later."

"That's stupid," I say, "He wouldn't go anywhere without me."

Still, that scares me, and I get a sick feeling in my stomach, and start sniffling. I can't imagine my life without my father, I'll start getting nothing but twos and threes at school. I'll even leave school and just go to the dogs. I get good marks at school purely for my father's sake, so he'll be pleased. Left to my own, a three would do me. And it would be enough for Mama as well. She looks at it this way: "A three equals 'Satisfactory', so that means the State is satisfied."

"I'm going to divorce him", says Mama.

"On what grounds?"

"He doesn't help me. I'm earning my own living. And I have to stand in queues, and drag home the shopping by myself."

"Was it different before?"

"No, it's always been like that."

"So why didn't you divorce him earlier, ten years ago?"

"I wanted to safeguard your childhood."

"So, when I was little, and knew nothing, you wanted to safeguard my childhood. And now, when I'm grown up, you want to deprive me of the person closest to me. That's treacherous of you."

"Well, so what?"

"So what nothing. I won't count for anything with you either."

"You've got your whole life ahead of you. But I want to be happy too."

I can't understand how, at the age of thirty, with a child, she can possibly want some other kind of happiness for herself. But it would be tactless to say that. So I say:

"Where have you ever seen people that were a hundred per cent happy? Look at Aunt Nina, she's five years younger than you, and ten kilos lighter, but she's got no husband and travels to work every day on two kinds of transport, an hour and a half just to get there. And she works in some sort of chemical engineering plant. Whereas you work just across the road, you love your job, and everybody respects you. You've found your own place in life. So that's fifty per cent already. I've turned out a good child, healthy and well-developed mentally. That's another forty-five per cent. And you're not suffering from anything - that's one per cent. So you're already ninety-six per cent happy. That leaves four per cent. And where have you ever seen anybody a hundred per cent happy? Name even one."

Mama doesn't say anything, she's thinking. But the fact is, nobody's happy a hundred per cent. There's something rattling in every little hut. Or as the English say, there's a skeleton in every cupboard. However Mama isn't consoled by other people's happiness deficiencies. She would rather have her missing four per cent than the first fifty. She sits down on my bed, shivering like an orphan. I say, "Lie down beside me."

She gets in beside me under the blanket. Her feet are cold, and she plants them on my legs, typically selfish. But I put up with it. Her tears are dropping into my eyes. I put up with that as well. I love her very much. My whole inside is aching with love. But I know if I start feeling sorry for her, she'll get even more mawkish. So I say, "Go and take a look at yourself in the mirror in daylight. What more do you need, apart from Papa and me? You should live for us."

Actually, to tell the truth, I think a person has to be selfish.

Career-minded and self-centred. In order to get on. Because if he's doing well, then the people around him benefit also. But if things are going badly for somebody, it's pretty grim for the others. I mean, if a person's getting a roasting, you don't see his nearest and dearest jumping for joy exactly. There's a faint scraping sound, it's Papa turning the key carefully in the lock, so as not to waken us. Then he enters the hall on tiptoe, stands still a few moments, obviously taking his coat off. He tiptoes into his own room too, with the floorboards creaking accusingly. Granny once said Papa had never found himself. And when he's going around on tiptoe like that, it seems to me he's searching for himself, with the light off, peering into every corner. And I feel terribly sorry for him. What if I reach forty and haven't found myself either, and don't know what to do with my life?

Hearing Papa's footsteps, Mama stirs and snuggles into my shoulder, breathing on my cheek. I put my arms round her and hold her tight, like a precious object. I lie awake thinking, if only she would put on weight. . . I can't wait till my parents start aging and getting stout - who'll want them when they're old and fat? Only each other, and me. Meanwhile they're still rushing around like mad, slim, wearing jeans. I sometimes think they've each got one foot nailed to the ground, while they're trying to run in different directions with the other. But where can you escape to with one foot nailed down? What's more, it seems to me that if they had both feet free, they'd be confused and wouldn't know what to do with their freedom, and would end up running to each other, because they do love each other, even if they don't realise it.

Incidentally, Lenka's mother has no husband at all, and

three children - all by different fathers - an old blind Granny, two kittens and a puppy. Yet it's always noisy and chaotic in their house, great fun. Maybe it's because Lenka's mama hasn't got the time to brood. When people have time on their hands, that's when they start thinking, And once they start thinking, well, they're bound to reach some sort of conclusion.

One day about a year ago a little boy on our street fell under a car. Everybody ran up to see how he was, but I dashed straight home. I was terribly frightened, not for myself, but for my parents. I'm still afraid even now: if something should happen to me - if I fall under a car, or grow up and get married. Who will I be leaving them for? And what are they going to do without me?

Zagoruiko has gone up to Marya Yefremovna and handed in his notebook. Most likely his happiest day will be when the Beatles get together again. Zagoruiko knows all the contemporary foreign groups: *Kiss, Queen, Boney M.* And all I know is: "Beethoven was a plebeian, with no private means. . . ", Schumann's Serenade from the music, and a few bits by ear.

I look at the clock. Sixteen minutes remaining. No time to ponder, or else they'll give me a two, and I won't get promoted to the ninth grade. I've decided to write about how we planted trees round the school. I read somewhere that each person in his life ought to plant a tree, raise a child, and write a book about the times he lived in. I recalled how I had to drag a full bucket of topsoil, to empty into the hole and give the tree a better chance to root. Zaguruiko came up and offered to help: "I'll give you a hand". I refused. "I'll manage," I said, and carried on dragging the bucket.
  Later I tipped the soil out into the hole and unclenched my fists. The handle of the bucket had left its mark on my palms - a deep blue weal. My shoulders were aching, and I even had a pain in my guts.
  "I'm exhausted," I announced with tragic dignity to the others standing around.

"I knew you would be," said Zagoruiko with malicious glee. "First she puts on airs, and now she'll start bragging about it."

I can't stand that Zagoruiko. He says whatever he thinks, despite the fact that people get an upbringing precisely in order to conceal their true feelings. Or at least whenever they would be out of place.

But no matter what happened there, the tree put down roots and will remain for future generations. So that means Marya Yefremovna will give me a five for content and I very rarely make any mistakes. I have innate literacy.

I look at the clock again. Eleven minutes to go. I give my pen a shake - mine has an ordinary nib, not a ballpoint - and start writing about the day Papa and I went to the cinema, and afterwards drove out to Granny's. And Mary Yefremovna can give me whatever she likes. They're not going to make an egoist or a career woman out of me anyway. I'll just live like all the others. I wrote that the film was terribly funny, with Louis de Funes playing the lead, and we giggled so much that people started turning round, and somebody rapped on my back with a walking stick, as if on a door. And it was the same as always at Granny's. We sat in the kitchen eating fish, which was really delicious. But it wasn't just the meal, it was the whole situation. They all loved me, and openly admired me. And I love them all too, one hundred per cent, and that in itself was of great benefit to them.

I have Papa's eyes, and Papa has Granny's eyes, hazel, with peaked eyebrows. We sat looking at each other with the same eyes, and feeling the same things. And we were like a tree: Granny the roots, Papa the trunk, and me the branches, reaching out to the sun.

And it was inexpressibly wonderful.

Of course, it wasn't the happiest day of my life. Simply happy. I haven't had my happiest day yet. That's still to come.

Black Murdo
Angus Watson

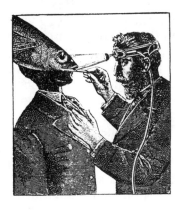

Murchadh Dubh an Taillear - Black Murdo the Tailor - was not a pious man. More a blasphemer many would have said. But as he came over the brow of the hill and saw what he had been hoping for, he murmured his thanks to the Lord. Below him was the sea, with a narrow strip of habitable land rising in terraces from the stony shore towards the foot of the hill on which he stood. The sea was leaden-hued and heavy with sullen waves, and the land covered by bent grass and bracken, yet the sight brought a laugh to his lips, and turning to face the way he had come he shouted "This is the place. I've found it. It's as I told you."

A little way down the pass a woman, grey before her time, stopped to look up at him, barely raising her head as if unable to believe that the spot where her man stood was indeed the top of the pass and not another curve in the hill's flank, hiding yet another weary curve behind it. A bundle across her shoulders, she led a garron weighed down seemingly to breaking point by a charred ridge pole lashed more or less in balance across his brown back. Beside the pony a girl of about twelve years came to a halt along with her mother, keeping her hand on the end of the timber to steady it as she had done through the three days of walking. Behind them a stocky black cow and two calves halted in their turn, as did a slightly older girl driving them. The girls looked for the hundredth time at one of the calves and wondered where it had come from. Had they not seen their own cow give birth? And her with only the one calf, until the day of turmoil seventy-two hours ago when the factor's men had come and burned and beaten down their houses along with all the others in the green glen, and tipped into the river all the seed corn they could find. But when Murdo had led their mother and themselves into the hills with their few rescued belongings, there had been two calves.

"Come on" Black Murdo shouted "We're there. I've got you there." He turned away from them again as they began to climb, the older girl prodding the weary cattle with her stick as she followed to the top of the *bealach*. As they joined Murdo at the summit the sun broke through the cloud, the sea turned blue and the red grass on the land they were eyeing glowed almost richly. "Seaweed for manure," Murdo murmured, " and could I only get my hands on a trim wee boat there'll be plenty fish to be had"; and leaving them to follow he set off downwards through the heather.

The first days were hard. Until Murdo had built a shelter of driftwood they slept in their plaids under the stars or the clouds or the rain, as they had done during their three day journey. But at least it was less cold here than on the high passes, though only the cattle and the garron fed middling well, knee-deep in the rough grass. Even so one of the calves died. They lived off it as long as they could, then on shellfish the girls gathered and on the few fish Murdo

managed to catch in the trap he built on the shore - a
U-shaped wall of stones with its open end to landward and
from which the receding tide could escape, leaving any fish
behind. With no cooking pot, Anna, the mother stood
stones in the smoky fire, and when they were as hot as she
could get them, she lay the food on them to warm through.
Worst of all was the lack of tools, and time short before
planting would have to be done. To clear the ground they
tethered the cow for a time then shifted her on a few yards.
The turf she had grazed down and dunged a little Murdo
hacked into squares with his knife, the only cutting edge
they had, and Anna turned over turf and shallow soil
together with a piece of wood. "It's lazy beds we'll be
making next year when I get tools."

"Lazy-beds or no, without a potato or an oat grain to
plant it's ourselves we'll be putting in the earth long before
next year. "

Murdo didn't answer, for there was no answer.

They laboured at the soil. Not to do so would be to admit
there was no hope. Then Murdo was away for two days,
coming back late on the second night carrying a piece of
cloth with its corners tied together and potatoes in it. "We'll
get not a speck more" he said when he showed them to the
others in the morning. And he went to plant them.

The girls had two pieces of hide from the dead calf. With
the edges drawn up with plaited strips of the same hide these
served as a milking pail or to fetch water in. Once the cow
was milked, if the tide was too small for gathering shellfish,
Anna *Bheag* and Mairead her sister would huddle beneath
the shelter and talk in low voices about the glen they had
been driven from, and where already in memory all was
happiness. Or they would run part way up the hill and back
just to get warm. On a day of days, Mairead, the younger
girl, came racing down the hill that lay to the south of their
dwelling place. "Mother, mother, there's a man, and him
coming this way!"

And when they turned to the south they saw him coming
down from the hill towards them. Shading their eyes against
the midday sky, they saw that he wore a green frock coat,

grey breeches and long woollen stockings and what
surprised them in such country, light shoes of leather. At
the neck of his linen shirt he wore a silk kerchief and when
he drew close they saw that his face was tanned and his hair
grey beneath his bonnet .

"It's a fine day that's in it" he cried as he halted before
them. He was the first living soul they had seen since the
factor's men had abused them. Murdo on his journey for
the potatoes had seen no habitation for many miles around.
And so they greeted him cautiously though politely. "I see
you have no house yet. Come."

And he led them to a spot they had passed many times
but where they had never before noticed a great quantity of
stone among the grass.

"The walls are as they fell after the people were driven
away. The byre as well." He pushed the grass away with his
foot to show them charred wood. "You brought a ridge pole
with you I see."

"You have sharp eyes on you" Murdo said with a quick
glance at Anna.

The stranger smiled. "I mean no harm." And turning
towards the sea: "Perhaps you will find more timber washed
up on the shore, over near the point." With a cheerful
"*Beannachd leibh*", he left them.

With the wind blowing their hair and pressing their
clothing hard against their thighs, they watched him go, then
looked more closely among the grass. It was as if the walls
of the house had fallen outwards, laying down each course
of stone roughly in line. Even the position of the doorway
could be made out from the patterns of spread out masonry.
"We'll not be long building this" Murdo said, and Anna, as
she looked about her, picturing the house that was to be,
looked less careworn than for many a day. The girls skipped
and danced on the old house floor, found peat ash among
the grass and squabbled about where the stool would stand
and which of them would cook.

The walls were indeed soon rebuilt - the stones seemed
light for their size - and there was indeed timber near the

point which they could use to form the skeleton of a roof. In a few days the frock coated man came again, bringing a peat-iron, and Murdo was able to open up an old peat bank on the hill - not without wondering who had last cut peat there, and when - and bring down turf as a roof covering until they would have dry rushes or a crop of straw for thatch.

Later, the frock coated man brought them a bag of oats, another day a cooking pot. He seemed to sense each small thing they needed and rarely came empty handed. The girls kept watch and they would study his lanky bonneted silhouette as it appeared over the hill, to try to make out what he carried on his shoulder or under his oxter. Murdo, glad to accept his gifts, was yet on his guard, afraid to believe such kindness did not conceal some danger or would not lead him into some kind of dependency. Anna accepted with simple gratitude for she acknowledged to herself that without the stranger's help they could not have survived. "How can we repay you?" she said one day.

"It is nothing" replied the frock coated man with a smile. "It pleases me that people are living here again."

Spring turned into Summer. The few oats and potatoes they had planted looked set to yield abundantly. The cow kept coming into season and should have been put in calf long ago; but where would they have found a bull in this place? Nevertheless her milk did not dry up and they felt the unlimited grazing and the suckling of her calf must have something to do with this. "The frock coated man brings us luck" Anna said, and Murdo could not deny it. He hardly felt uneasy at all now as he watched him giving the girls some trinket he had brought or telling them stories of Fionn or the fairy folk. But where did he come from? There was no house nearby, Murdo was sure, and yet he had brought them a smouldering peat, in the time-honoured fashion, for the first kindling of the fire he sat beside now. They asked no questions of the stranger - and a stranger he still was to them. They did not wish to offend by appearing inquisitive, nor by some blunder to shatter the benign spell the man seemed to cast over their life. They were only too happy to accept the situation as it was. Like travellers stranded in mist on an icy ridge they feared that any move might destroy the fine balance that kept them precariously alive.

As the days grew longer the frock coated man took to coming in the evening so as not to keep them from the work of the day. And as their immediate needs became less he brought fewer practical things, like a *caschrom* or gut or a pair of hens, and took to singing them songs of the seal people or of the joy and heartbreak of love, or telling them stories of the giants and heroes of old times who sleep away the years, who knows how many, until their some-time resurrection. One night he came with a fiddle and after that the evening often rang with the sound of reels as the girls danced on the grass or slow sad airs would echo in the dim interior of the house, mingling with the peat reek as it rose to the roof.

With the stranger's help Murdo had fashioned a *curach* from driftwood covered with the rest of the calf's hide, and the fish he caught from it had become an important part of their feeding. Late one day he was fishing near the point. Ready to give up for the night after some hours without success, he was about to pull in his net for the last time when he heard a voice calling to him from the rocks. "Put down your net over here, *a Mhurchaidh*, and see what you'll get."
     The man standing by the water's edge looking down into the foam was stocky and dark-haired, dressed in black clothing and a low-crowned hat. He looked somewhat like a minister, or so Murdo thought. Where his finger pointed, true enough, the surface of the water seemed to boil, as when a shoal of herring comes into a sea loch. So Murdo paddled his way clumsily over towards the rocks and cast his net into the bubbling sea. Immediately it was filled with a great weight, but as Murdo began to heave it on board, something gave way and he was hurled, like a landed fish himself, into the shallow water at the dark man's feet, still managing to hang onto the rim of the curach which overturned on top of him. Net and paddle were lost. The

dark man, bellowing with laughter, dragged the precious *curach* and the floundering Murdo onto the rocks, where he dumped them and watched the water stream from both of them back into the ocean. After a few moments, still laughing, he pulled Murdo to his feet, throwing an arm round his shoulders.

"*Tiugainn a bhalaich*. Let's get you home and dry."

After the day of Murdo's soaking the dark man came often to "*ceilidh* on them" as he called it. He came as regularly as the frock coated man but somehow never at the same time. On a fine day, he would turn up around mid-morning bringing tobacco and clay pipes, or whisky in a pot, and he and Murdo would sit in the sunshine and smoke or drink, or both, and the work of the land would wait while he talked and laughed and Murdo mostly listened. At other times he would sit in the house and tease the giggling girls about a hair-ribbon or keekin-glass or some other gee-gaw he had brought them. "It's garters he'll be bringing you next day" said Murdo with a smirk - he had a good drink in him - but Anna was black offended and only hid the extent of her outrage out of deference to their visitor.

"Tell me, *a Mhurchaidh*" said the dark man one day, "Why do they call you Black Murdo the Tailor?"

There was hoeing needing done and hay to be cut and thatching to be done while the weather held, but it was pleasant in the sunshine and the dark man was generous with his tobacco and Murdo didn't like to offend a stout drinking companion. So he told how, many years back, he had been up among the high bens one day, when he had chanced upon a band of men from his own glen coming back from a cattle raid. They had got no cattle for seemingly there had been a skirmish and it had gone badly with them. Some of them were beyond help and would never make it home, but one youth had a gash in his belly which didn't look too bad and Murdo had sewn it up with a needle and thread.

"He died anyway, the poor man, and I never lived down

the neatness they said was in my stitching. It's the Tailor they were calling me after that."

The dark man was greatly amused by the story. "Well now, *a Mhurchaidh*, I'm wondering were you too clever a fellow to get caught in the fighting and is that why you were in one piece when you 'chanced upon' your friends?"

"Ach no" protested Murdo. "I was never one for the cattle thieving at all."

"*Cha chreid mi gun robh*! I don't believe you were!" roared the dark man.

When the frock coated man came now he could see changes. A flattened patch of oats where the cow had been allowed to wander, or a torn net lying by the door unmended. The girls seemed less eager to listen to his stories or dance to his fiddle and he could almost have believed they were sniggering at him now when his back was turned. Anna's ways were as welcoming as ever but she looked weary, and she dropped her eyes if she saw his gaze rest on the ragged thatch or the overgrown potato bed. From that time on his visits became less frequent.

The dark man for his part began to stay even longer as if taking to himself the time that had been the frock coated man's. The year was wearing on and the work was so far behind that Murdo himself grew anxious now and he and Anna would leave the dark man seated by the fire, apologising that he would have only the girls for company.

"No, no, *a chairdean*, I would be the last to keep a body back from winning his bread from the ground. And these lassies and I get on just fine, don't we?"

And he would laugh, and the girls would giggle, and Murdo and Anna would hurry out to try to salvage something from the work which had started so well in the Spring.

It was one such evening, with the parents working some way from the buildings and the dark man and the girls inside, that the frock coated man walked into the house. He stood still for an instant as his eyes adjusted to the change of light. Then he made out the dark man, with the girls on his lap. As recognition dawned they heard him murmur to himself: "Now I understand." And he saw the hair on the knuckles of a thick-fingered hand standing out black against the white flesh of a thigh.

"He's going to marry us. He's going to marry us" chanted the sisters.

The dark man surged to his feet, sweeping the girls from his knee as he made for the frock-coated man. But Mairead in her fall overturned the board and the whisky jug with it, and a trail of spirit spread like a fuse as far as the burning peats. It sizzled for a moment then burst into flame, catching the rushes on the floor. As the men struggled, the blaze spread to the blanket which closed off the box bed and this took it straight to the thatch. Then there was no hope of saving the house.

Murdo and Anna were alerted by the girls' screaming. As they dragged them clear before the roof fell, in their last vision, stained blood-red by the flames, was of the frock coated man held by the throat against the wall while the dark man's fist beat him unceasingly about the head.

Murdo stood, a hissing at his feet as whisps of burning thatch came gently to rest on the damp ground. His womenfolk clung to each other a few paces away.

"My father used to talk about a place in Moidart where there was plenty land. Maybe we'd be able to settle there before the winter comes?"

Heads Or Tails
J. N. Reilly

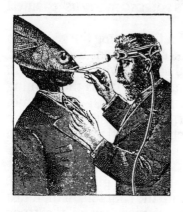

J im was nine years old. It was summertime and the
streets were parched and dusty. Frank, a boy of
thirteen who lived in the next tenement, had asked
him if he would like to go to the woods with him, that
Bert and maybe a few other boys would be going, and
then they would go to the river.

Frank looked like a monkey, and could have been
regarded as completely simian if it had not been for his eyes,
for his gaze was definitely human, mischievous but devious.
There was something predatory, even cruel about Frank's
look, which meant that Jim was a little afraid of him and
never sought him out as a playmate. However, on this
occasion as on those previous rare occasions when he had
decided to play with Frank, Jim, being the uncluttered child
he was, had forgotten that Frank could be scary and usually

ultimately unsettling. But first he had to get his mother's permission to go with Frank and Bert to the woods which were a good half mile away. He wasn't going to mention the river for, even although it had been a long hot summer and the level of the river was low, just the mention of it would set her imagining him drowned and bemoaning it would be her fault if he were to drown and folk would say she had neglected him. Nonetheless she hummed and hawed, saying that Frank and Bert were scruffy, dirty and always up to no good, and she didn't want the police at her door because a son of hers was in trouble. Jim ingratiatingly agreed that Frank and Bert weren't the best boys but they weren't really that bad either. He promised he would behave, that he wouldn't do anything wrong, and what could happen anyway? He knew she would give her permission, and she did, whereas his father wouldn't have, but he was at work. So Frank and he set off along the street to meet Bert who was waiting with a group of about six or seven boys, all schoolmates. The boys were older than Jim and after the summer holidays were to begin their second year at secondary school.

The tenements sweating in the heat, the boys talked of football and girls, especially a girl called Agnes. While listening to them, Jim fell to thinking of an incident when he couldn't have been more than five years old and was behind the settee with the girl from downstairs. She was five or six years old herself. He could hear her father and his mother speaking as he caressed the soft flesh and mysterious slit between her legs. One moment she was holding her pants down for him to look and feel, the next she was pushing him away and trying to get out from behind the settee, but putting up no resistance as he pulled her back. As this went on, the only sound was of their parents talking. Jim and the girl didn't utter a sound. But then:
What are you two doing behind there? came the gruff accusing voice of her father. Come on, get out of there. Out.

Jim recalled the tremendous wave of guilt and shame which pervaded him at the sound of this voice.

The boys shouted, laughed and cursed insouciantly as they crossed the fields, the tenements receding into the distance exhilarating them with freedom from parents. Dumb-eyed cows stared over barbed wire at their noise, and leaving the field for the road by the farmhouse, the pungent smell of manure attacked their nostrils. Some of them danced around, jumping up and down, holding their noses and twisting their faces. Others screamed towards the farmhouse, to the trees, to the hedgerows, to the sky:

Your farm smells of shit. Do you hear me? Hey ...

shitey bastards.

Who stood on the fuckin shit, own up.

Keep your bicycle clips on.

It's Bobby ... hey Bert ...

Their voices rang out in the clear blue, joyously mingling with the bird-song and the throb of distant car engines. They ran onto the bridge and pitched stones into muddy water below. Frank and Bert with an enormous boulder between them called out, One, two, three, now ... and hurled it into the water, but here was no big splash. The river was shallow here. The boulder protruded from the surface of the water, shining wet in the sunshine, reptilian. They soon tired of throwing stones and went to the bank in the damp shadow of the bridge, where all sorts of garbage had been dumped. It was a morass of weeds, piles of food cans, beer cans faded wrappers, broken bricks and smashed bottles glimmering amongst newspapers and fungi. The boys searched for unbroken bottles to smash but couldn't find any. They raked through the garbage for any treasures that were maybe hidden from view, but found nothing but a collage of economics and entropy. They stepped into the sunlight and ran for the next bridge. This one hung over the railway tracks. The old church steeple towered from behind the trees rising into the summer blue the sound of a train coming. There was a mad rush to the wall of the bridge, and obscene gestures and curses thrown at the driver in the deafening roar as the train sped under the bridge and raced off to another world.

Have you got a girlfriend? One of Bert's friends asked Jim.

He was about to lie and say yes, but: No, he replied. Frank knew he didn't have a girlfriend anyway. The boy didn't say another word to him, but turned and shouted: Let's see your balls Bert. Come on, give them some air. Give us a show.

Swivelling his hips and wiggling his arse, Bert revealed an enormous pair of testicles. A whip of laughter and applause went up.

Make them bigger, shouted Frank spluttering in laughter, that suspect look in his eyes.

Bert cradled his balls and began gently patting them. Delicate pink bouncing to cheers as they grew as large as two small apples, as if they had been pumped full of air. Jim was amazed by the enormity of these testicles, so pink and smooth with blond hair.

Make them bigger, Frank called again.

That's as far as they'll go, Bert replied, still gently patting them and thrusting his hips back and forth. The sound of a car engine could be heard approaching. Bert hurriedly stuffed his balls away. The boys ran giggling to the side of the road, laughing in the knowledge that the driver didn't have a clue of their goings-on. The car safely out of sight, Frank implored Bert to show his balls again.

No. Come on, we'll thieve some rhubarb from the church garden.

Oh Bert, show us your balls again, Frank pleaded.

I can't be bothered, said Bert, Maybe after.

He wiped his nose with the palm of his hand.

I don't feel like going. I'll wait here for you, Jim called to Bert. He didn't want to get involved in anything that might bring trouble.

I'll stay with Jim, said Frank. We'll see you later.

The other boys followed Bert and disappeared round the top of the road.

We'll go to the bridge and wait for them, said Jim.

No, we'll go and rest under the trees, said Frank. If that's okay with you. It'll be cooler there.

Yes. Sure.

Back down the road a few metres, they climbed over the barbed wire fence and made their way down a grassy slope till they found a suitable place to stretch out. Well hidden from view from the road, they lay gazing into the rustling vault of verdure above them, spattered here and there with the blue of the sky, trickling with white sun light. Distant voices drifted to them, a dog barked in the farmyard. It was beautifully still and cool, Frank lay on his side and took a carving knife from under his sweater and started playing with it, sticking it into the earth. Staring into Jim's eyes, he said, Bert's got some size of balls hasn't he?

Yes.

Did you get a hard-on when Bert was showing his balls?

No, Jim replied, enjoyably and furtively feeling the fear rippling through him like a sea breeze as he felt his prick swell.

Have you got a hard-on now, Jim?

Frank's eyes looked as if about to drip out of his face and onto the grass. Leaning forward he poked between Jim's legs with the tip of the knife.

Yes. Jim replied, knowing it would be futile to lie, that he couldn't conceal the fact.

Take it out and have a wank. I don't mind, Frank whispered, his voice hoarse, eyes unblinking.

No. I don't feel like it.

In truth Jim had never masturbated.

Take it out and rub it. You'll feel better.

Frank's smile stretched into a sly grin.

No. I don't want to. I'm going home.

We don't need to go home now. We can stay a while longer, said Frank annoyed.

I'm going home now. Jim stood up and made for the road.

Okay, okay. I'll walk you home, said Frank angrily, putting his knife away. They walked in silence, Frank glowering all the way. They parted at the corner of their block at Frank's close.

See you Frank.

Yes, see you, said Frank churlishly.

When Jim pushed open the door of his house, he was met with his mother's voice.

Where have you been? Did you go to the river?

We went to the old bridge and steeple.

He went straight to the living-room and switched on the television.

Don't go back out, his mother shouted from the kitchen. Your tea's nearly ready.

The image of Roadrunner flashed onto the screen. He loathed that cartoon. Ignoring the picture and the sound, he lay back in the chair and relaxed, feeling like Indiana Jones after a day of courage in the face of hopeless odds against savage natives. And Frank had been one of those ferocious natives who had attacked with spears and long shining knives. However, he didn't dwell on his fantastic commingling of the days earlier events, for he was soon picturing the dark-haired girl who lived round the corner. He saw her crossing the busy road, wearing black trousers and brilliant red sweater. He got lost in every soft lubricious curve from her breasts to her buttocks to her thighs, the way she walked, the way she flicked her hair into place. There wasn't a flaw in her beauty. He felt his prick grow. He imagined being with her in a shady spot by the river. Just about to make love with her ... he rose from his chair, went along the hall past his mother in the kitchen, and went into the bathroom. Snibbing the door behind him, he pulled down his trousers. He had to find out. He sat down on the edge of the bath, but leapt off swiftly, the enamel was freezing cold. He placed a towel beneath his buttocks and began to caress his prick. He watched it grow. He surveyed the delicate blue veins in white flesh. The bathroom was wonderfully cool and fresh. The sun lit the window and stretched across the wall. He could hear children laughing and shouting and adults talking on the street below. But nothing was happening. He kept caressing, growing disappointed that no wonderful thing had happened. But then. He felt a strange sensation deep in his belly. He began to feel afraid but moved his hand faster. The sensation grew. He couldn't stop himself. He felt as if his belly was aflame. Thousands of freezing silver arrows raced through his veins. He moved his hand even faster. The sensation was reaching such an excruciating level that to go on any longer he felt something terrible would happen. Suddenly he gasped for air as if in a car that had suddenly accelerated. He didn't know if he was feeling pain or pleasure. He grabbed his belly and doubled towards the floor, afraid he'd damaged himself and would have to get his mother to take him to hospital. What have I done? Should I shout for my mother. Oh no ... clutching his belly, he moaned and ejaculated. Semen spurted into the air, spattered on to the wall, onto his legs, the toilet, and dripped down the immaculate white enamel of the cistern.

He sat on the floor to catch his breath before setting about cleaning up the mess. His feelings were ambivalent at first, did he or didn't he like what had happened, but when he had calmed down he laughed at his stupidity in thinking he might have damaged himself, and he knew that what he had experienced was pleasure. He would do it again, he had to, and again and again and again.

Making Hay
Wilma Murray

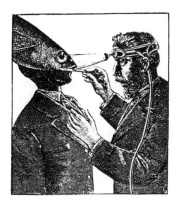

E veryone who is old enough to remember has a tale to
tell about the summer of seventy six. They might tell
you about the ladybird plague, how complete
strangers would stand and pick the insects off one
another in queues and shops in intimate grooming
sessions. They will tell you about the friendships they made
waiting to carry water from the stand pipes in the street and
if they are old enough, compare it to wartime. That summer
changed many insignificant lives in small but significant
ways. It certainly changed mine.

In this particular part of the country that summer is
remarkable for ever having happened at all. This is a corner
of the globe where good weather is mostly an accident, the
result of some high pressure system straying a little further
west or north than usual and remaining strong enough to
resist the billiard-ball activity of lows scudding in across the
Atlantic two or three times a week. This is a place of rowdy

skies where in a lifetime of weather the number of cloudless shimmering days adds up to perhaps one decent summer by global standards. So, there is no easy habit of outdoor living here, rather a mad scramble on the odd good day to pack a summer into one afternoon, having wasted the morning in doubt of it lasting.

But in seventy six, the blue days went on and on. People learned to ration their greed for the sun after overdosing in the early days. In our street we began to speak to our neighbours again, out in the gardens. After the long, pale and private existence indoors, we had forgotten half their names. Anyway, the men looked so different in shorts and sandals, bare to their waists on ladders or behind mowers. Even Dad hauled his belly into an old pair of shorts he had once used for squash.

Mum's response to the wonderful weather was to wash blankets, a typical repressed woman's response, I informed her. I had just discovered the woman's movement and was heavily into feminist books that summer. She seemed to me to be a walking example of what the books were preaching against. Seeing her with her hair dark and lank with sweat and her thick doughy arms struggling with the heavy pile of wet blankets, I can remember my anger rising, though, to be honest, whether it was born of guilt or embarrassment or genuine concern is harder to recall.

"You should be taking it easy on a day like this," I told her.

"We weren't all born to be ladies like you, missy."

"We should go somewhere."

"You please yourself, but I'm certainly not going to waste a day like this. I could get all the beds turned if this keeps up." She loosened the top buttons of her blouse, dried the sweat from the back of her neck with the tail of her apron and blew down between her breasts.

"For God sake get some of those clothes off."

She looked me over in my bikini and smiled the half smile she had used a lot on me that summer. "Don't get that chair all oily."

When the blankets were at last on the line, she sat down, kicked her feet free of her slippers and pulled her skirt up over her knees... "Reminds me of France this."

"When were you ever in France?"

"Long before your time, missy." I remember she said it then got up and went back into the house, leaving me with a changed map of my mother's life which I contemplated and found uncomfortable.

Then she bought a swimsuit. It was absolutely hideous, splattered with bright orange flowers and built like scaffolding. Back from College one day I found her in this thing in front of the long mirror in my room.

"Well?" she asked. "What do you think?"

"I think it's horrible."

"So do I, actually. But it was cheap. It was in a sale."

"I can see why. You're not going to go out in that, are you?"

"Oh, it'll do. It's only for the garden."

In this monstrous costume, she prostrated herself before the sun alongside me one Saturday afternoon. I could not reasonably complain, but as I turned from time to time to get as even a tan as possible, I would catch sight of her great thighs, dimpled with fat and threaded with little purple veins and I would pray fervently never to let myself get like her.

The thing was, she took on this fantastic colour. Starting with a pale honey gold, her skin, without much help from all of my expensive oils and lotions, darkened to a deep rich brown which made me look ill by comparison, in spite of my marathon efforts on the lounger. I admit it suited her. Dad certainly thought so. They smiled more at each other that summer and reminisced about other summers I had never known existed, laughing in unison before sentences ended in a two-way conspiracy of memories from which I was excluded by reason of not having been born at the time. For the first time, I had to give some thought to them as a couple.

One lunch time, I came back and found them in bed together. What shocked me was not that they were clearly enjoying themselves, but the stark white of mother's backside against the brown of her legs and back, obscene as a baboon's bum. They turned and stared, startled into silence but were giggling again by the time I slammed the door.

Things were never the same after that. She became smug and I became vicious. I attacked her figure, her age, her hair, her clothes and her ideas. I accused her of neglecting the house for the selfishness of sunbathing. She smiled her smile and tipped my own arguments neatly back into my lap, without anger, even quoting back at me passages from the books I had been forcing on her for her re-education.

I began to wish for the summer to end, but the sun went on shining. I watched my mother turning into a hussy for the sun, splaying her legs shamelessly on the sunbed, even exposing her wilted tits. She began getting up earlier and earlier in the morning, often stripping my bed almost from under me in an attempt to get things done before the best of the day started. The sun seemed to have turned her mind.

"I'm looking for a flat to share with friends in the autumn term." I announced to her one day in the garden. She did not even open her eyes. "I suppose you'll be glad to get rid of me. Then you can lie out here all day every day without feeling guilty."

"If you say so." She still did not open her eyes.

The weather broke at last towards the middle of September. I greeted the cool autumn days with relief. We went bramble picking as a family, like always, and made jam and pies for the freezer like any other year. I began to regret my decision to leave. I saw things as having got back to normal and was relieved. Mum and I began to chat over the supper dishes the way we had done before. I stopped criticising everything she did and said, but if she noticed she showed little sign. Now and again she smiled that odd smile of hers.

As my spirits rose, Mum's seemed to fall. She grew quiet and restless and spent a lot of time at the dining room window staring out, saying nothing. Dad hugged her a lot

and made notable efforts to cheer her up. He bought her a
sun lamp for her birthday when she began to lose the lustre
of her tan. She liked that.

"I do miss the sun," she said, when she kissed him thank
you. "It's the first summer I've enjoyed for, oh, years and
years."

"We could go back to Juan les Pins next year if you like,"
he said to her one day at lunch. "Just the two of us."

My attention was alerted. "What about me? Don't I rate
an invite?"

"You're too old to be trailing along with us now, aren't
you? Anyway, your mother deserves a break."

"A break? She's done nothing all summer but lie around
on her fat ..."

"That's enough!" He had not raised his voice to me for
years.

"No. It's not enough. Not nearly enough." I said much
more than I should have done. I let go and flung the whole
rotten summer back at the two of them, tears snarling up
my words and ending with an uncontrollable fit of hiccups.

"Look. We know you're maybe a bit upset about leaving
home and all that, but there's no need to speak like...."

"Upset? Upset? Don't you kid yourselves. I just can't
wait to get out of here. To get shot of you two. You make
me want to puke, the pair of you."

My mother was in tears when I left the table. I felt a
fierce and powerful joy at the hurt I knew I had inflicted. I
packed and left that afternoon without speaking to either
of them, too afraid to look at their faces. I did not even leave
them an address. I waited five weeks before I even phoned
and in all that time they never once tried to contact me.

That's how I remember seventy six. It was the year I ran
away from home. I was nineteen, coming on twenty. I trailed
back, of course, and now I even go on holiday with them to
the villa which they rent every summer in the hills above
Grasse. I don't go every year, though. Its viciously hot there
in the summer and I must say I'm not as keen on the sun as
I used to be.

The Man Who Was To Blame
Alan Mason

1. Candy Floss Consultation

"No, no. My pleasure, dear boy."

"Which reminds me. How are things with Jean?"

"No better."

"The last time I saw you - "

"Ah well, Peter. The anticipation of the event, you know. I had high hopes."

"So the thin air of Tiahuananco didn't work the expected wonders?"

"This is a real treat. I haven't been to Coney Island in years. We must try the shooting galleries. Shall we discuss your patient?"

"Fine. We'll call him Mr. M."

"How intriguing. Am I meant to guess?"

"If you do I'll deny it."

"Very well. Mr. M it is."

"Suffice to say he was in business. Big business. The very top of the tree. Until 1974, when scandal forced him into premature retirement. Nothing proven, you understand."

"I understand. And his first attack. Within the year?"

"Yes. A big jump in his drinks bill, the usual signs."

"Was there any history of conscience?"

"None whatsoever. He's typical of the breed, Max. Never had a day's trouble in his life."

"Who attended?"

"Fitzpatrick. Well, you know how I feel about Fitzpatrick."

"I think you're too hard on the old boy. That paper you read at the institute. A bit strong, wasn't it? His treatment of the conscience-stricken. It's paid dividends in the past."

"The past, exactly. His methods are antiquated. I mean, how many more libraries does America need? Lord, it's his answer to everything."

"Philanthropy has eased many a rich man's burden."

"A library is a palliative. You taught me that, Max."

"And a library is what he prescribed for Mr. M?"

"No, actually. He suggested a dolphinarium. You know the kind of thing. The happy smiles on the faces of the little children."

"You see, Peter, he does try."

"The patient was not convinced. By the time I got to him, Mr. M's conscience had been plaguing him for nearly three years and he was a very sick man. He couldn't live with himself much longer. What was there to say? I gave him six months. At the outside."

"Now you're sure of this, Peter? It's understandable, you're anxious to defend your decision in the light of subsequent events. But a transplant. That was his only hope? You're certain?"

2. Blubber In A Car Park

"It's very narrow," said Harry Mercer. "You'll have to get out my side."

He turned off the engine and put the ignition key in his pocket. Then, without looking at her, he opened the door and stepped out.

"I must say you don't make things easy. What is it with you tonight?"

"OK, OK," he said, holding open the door, "give me your hand."

Sandy looked down, worried that her dress might catch. "No thanks," she said. "I'll manage."

He was leaning forward, but he suddenly straightened up, catching his head on the door.

"Oh shit."

He stumbled back into the car and fell against her shoulder. Someone played be-bop in his attic. He was blubbering into her gardenia.

"Hey, Harry. Come on, Harry. What is it? Tell me, honey."

He pulled himself up and sucked in the tears. He dabbed his eyes. "I'm sorry." She watched him.

"Come on," he said. He was steadying now. More like himself.

"Oh no." She opened the glove compartment. "We'll stay right here and talk about it."

"Well it's nothing. Really, Sandy, it's nothing."

"Sure. Here, grab a cup."

"I'm having a little bother with my conscience, that's all."

"You are what?" she said. "What do you mean?"

"It won't leave me alone right now."

"Wait a minute. Correct me if I'm wrong - but they gave you a new one, didn't they?"

"Gave? Bought, sweetheart. The clearest conscience money could buy. Look at me - I was promised a full and carefree retirement. Mr. Mercer, you'll be a new man."

"Griff Paterson - wasn't that the guy's name? The donor? Hey - are you alright? Do you want me to try and find a psychiatrist?"

"No, I'll be OK. Bastard."

"Please - I'm doing my best."

"No, Griff Paterson. He was 93 years old. A Canadian! A good age and a blameless life. They told me there was nothing on his mind. They had such wonderful affidavits from his family. He was a happy old bastard, oh yeh, died in his rocking chair without a care in the world, Jesus what those fucking doctors didn't know."

"Oh Lord," groaned Sandy. "Well let's have it, Harry.

What's bugging you? Paterson. Did he cheat on his wife - steal from the kid's piggy bank - what?"

3. Mountains Out Of Motels

"What are you doing?"
"I'm writing to my Congressman."
"Come to bed."
"There has to be an immediate freeze."
"Quite likely if you don't get in here."
She had turned down the bedsheets. Arranged herself to accomodate him.
"Hell, Harry, won't it keep? I mean, we've lasted this long."
No response.
"And a girl my age. She can't have too many good ones left to her. You wouldn't want it going to waste now, would you?"
There was no movement; no sound except the scratching of his pen on the toilet paper.
"OK, Harry, I can see you're serious."
She pulled up the sheets, flipped her chest back into her nightdress and picked up a magazine.
"I told you. I've got it on my conscience."
"No, Harry," she reminded him. "Not your conscience."
She came to the article that must have sparked him off. 'President Gets Go Ahead On MX'. That bastard Reagan was ruining her sex life. Maybe it had been a mistake to vote for him after all.
"You know, Sandy - "
Harry turned for a moment from his writing.
"I just don't understand it. This Griff Paterson - "
He waved his pen, referred to his head as he spoke the name.
"He never had a thing to do with it. Never dealt in heavy water or set atoms colliding. Never played a part in developing it. Didn't have a hand in dropping it. Never put a bolt in place or a fuse towards it. And yet it haunted him.

Christ, how it haunted him. And now, having paid through the nose for the privilege, it haunts me. I mean why?" He shook his head. "Why Sandy?"

She shrugged her shoulders.

"I've got his conscience. I've got that alright. But I haven't got the explanations to go with it. To me the bomb makes sense. It keeps the peace. Preserves the free market. Ensures a good standard of living and a Christian future for our children."

"Rah for our side."

"And yet Paterson feel guilty."

He scratched his head - with the wrong end of the pen, leaving a thin blue line along his temple. "Ah well," he said. "I'd better get this letter written. I want to catch the early post."

"Listen, Harry. If your brain tells you the bomb's OK. Well, can't you talk the old fart's conscience out of it? What am I saying? This from a girl who - Never mind that's another story. We've got to get you help."

"Help? Sure. An immediate freeze. That would help."

"Harry - that's nothing more than a salve. There has to be something more permanent. I mean, are we going to let this conscience, this lodger, this interloper, go on dictating to you?"

The silence returned. She threw down the magazine and switched on the radio. "Imagine there's no countries -"

"Jesus Christ."

She switched it off.

4. The Congressman Receives

"It's good of you to see me Congressman."

"Not at all, Mr. Mercer. My pleasure. Your company did me some mighty fine favours in the past. Though I confess," he unplugged his cigar, "I'm surprised to see you fronting an outfit like this -" The Congressman gestured to the button on Harry's lapel.

Nuclear Freeze Now.

"Me too," said Harry.

"Conscience pricking you in your old age?"

Harry looked around at the cardboard boxes, spilled from the corridor into the plush office.

"It's not my conscience," he said.

"No? Exercising it for a friend?"

"Hardly a friend. Anyway, Congressman, I'm obliged to you. You'll appreciate I'm here to present you with this petition. Over my dead body, you understand. Or rather, over a million signatures. Certified? Should be. They're all crazy. Every goddam one of them. However it has to be done. We have to have a freeze. Nuclear Freeze Now."

"If I may say so, Mr. Mercer you seem to be a trifle schizophrenic on this matter."

Harry sat down, slumped, in fact, onto a box full of signatures.

"You don't know the half of it, Congressman."

"Go ahead."

"The fact is, I bought a new conscience. Money down for a clean slate. Only it didn't turn out quite as expected. Contrary to indications, this guy Paterson - Griff Paterson, that's the donor - he was stacked to the roof and burdened down with guilt. It was the bomb he never wanted. Yet it was the bomb he was to blame for just as sure as if he'd built it with his own hands. It was the bomb that kept the peace and allowed him to work his farm. Yet it was the bomb that would take out his farm and his family and turn men to salt. It was the bomb that brought him to his knees in the middle of his yard among the shit and startled chickens. Hear me Lord!" (The Congressman took a step back.) "Never voted for it, Lord. Never meant for it to happen. Never endorsed or approved it. Never sanctioned any part of it. Always loved my enemies. But I built that monster. Sure as I'm on my knees in shit. I put my name on it, Lord, and the names of my family. I sat back there on my porch and I knew full well what was going on. What was firming up under the horizon. What my money was building and how my taxes were being spent. I sat back and let it happen, Lord. The responsibility is mine. I'm as guilty as the men who did it. An accessory before the fact. All the worse for being a thinking man with balls enough to do something about it."

Harry stood up. "Get the picture?"

"Quite."

"The guy was to blame. Now don't give me logic, Congressman. Don't give me common sense. I'm stuck with this thing. Chained to a conscience I never bargained for. Bugged into action and committed to a cause that gives me the heebies."

"I tell you what, Mr. Mercer. How about a word with the President? I think I could arrange that. He can be mighty persuasive."

"I don't need to be persuaded, Congressman. I know in my head what's what."

The Congressman drew on his cigar. His opinions he drew from his gut.

"How do you know it's the real thing? What I mean is. We've got some men of so-called conscience up on the Hill. Their conscience won't let them do this. Their conscience won't allow them to support that. In all conscience they can't go along with this. Conscience dictates. Conscience precludes. Conscience puts a finger up their ass. Conscience forbids any consideration of such-and-such a policy. Yet before you know it, they're lining up and voting with the President after all. In other words, Mr. Mercer, it's my experience that conscience is a piece of shit. No offence to yourself or Mr. Paterson."

"None taken, Congressman."

"So how about it? Put yourself in the hands of the Great Communicator. I tell you, that man knows from shit. You talk about conscience. There's the conscience of the nation. The fiery cross on our hilltops. The shining laser on our high frontier. I advise you, Mr. Mercer. Take your bearings from the President. Follow that light and sleep safe at the wheel."

5. *To The Stars*

"So what happened next? I heard your Mr. M went back to hospital. Not another transplant?"

"Not exactly. Well, in a way. Can I get you a drink, Max? Actually he decided to go without."

"Without a drink?"

"Without a conscience."

"Really? Well, that's the news. Thank you, Peter. It's probably for the best though, wouldn't you say? I mean, we seem to have managed along without one. Doesn't seem to have harmed us any. Indeed, had we been burdened with such a thing. Well, I dread to think of the consequences. Or rather the lack of them. Some ice in that?"

"No thanks. Which reminds me, I brought you the results of those tests. What say we give it a try?"

"We'll have to get round the Commission of course."

"Shouldn't be too difficult."

"I must say, these are very impressive, Peter. Real advances to be made here."

"I'm glad you like it, Max."

"I'll order up some chimps."

"Do."

"A couple of gross. To be going on with?"

"Yes. And some of those whatchamacallits. They come in handy."

"I'll get on it."

"To Progress, then."

"To Progress. Why not? Cheers, Peter."

"Cheers, Max."

Frieda
George Pryde

I t had rained early, before the men left for work at
seven, continuing through the morning. Parting the
curtain, Frieda gazed down at the vapour rising from
the hot, damp concrete. "It's stopped," she
murmured.

Frances leant forward, looking out. "Good, perhaps
we'll have some tennis tonight after all." She ran her fingers
lightly through Frieda's hair. "Doesn't she have beautiful
hair, Madge? Frieda, I just love how it sits on your
shoulders."

Her Boston drawl irritated Frieda who turned, shaking
her hair free. "Frances, you've had too much vodka, my
dear, you're embarrassing the girl." Madge flicked ash from
her skirt. Her four year old son, pale and limp from the heat,
lay on the couch with his head in her lap. Frieda shrugged.
"I must go, Wim will soon be home." She smiled. "Thank

you for the drink. I am not good company today."

"Don't be silly, Frieda, sit down!" said Madge, patting the couch with a long skeletal hand covered in gold rings. "You mustn't let Frances chase you away."

"Really, I must go."

In her flat she switched on the air conditioning, awakening Mohammed who was lying in the shade of the verandah, toes clinging to the railing, head down on his bare chest.

"Missie want?"

She shook her head. "Stay. Stay, Mohammed."

He glanced up at her, large eyed and uncomfortable. "I make you cup of coffee, tea?"

"No, nothing," said Frieda. "Just stay." She held up her hand and he settled again, uneasily. "Where is Nurul?"

"In the market, missie. You want me to -?"

"No, Mohammed, never mind." She returned to the living room. Wim would be in shortly. He'd have a whisky, then strip and shower. After dinner he would sit on the verandah and smoke a cigar while she listened to a tape. Later he would spread process diagrams on the table, cradling his head in his hands.

Nurul came in, smiling broadly. "Hello, Missie!" He went into the kitchen, closely followed by Mohammed. Frieda stepped onto the verandah and leant on the railing, listening to their laughter and the clattering of pots as they prepared dinner. Beyond the flats the silver columns of the chemical plant shimmered orange in the setting sun. In the grass below, children kicked a ball, their excited cries echoing through the compound.

The doorbell rang. She sighed, and entered the room again. Mohammed had opened the door.

"Mr Gordon, Missie," he said, retreating into the kitchen.

Frieda smiled, extending her hand. "Come in... won't you, Gordon. How are you?"

Henderson grinned. "Hi, Frieda!"

"Won't you have a drink?"

"A beer would be great." He loosened his shirt and flapped the ends about. His body was tanned a deep bronze.

Frieda looked away. "Mohammed, a beer for Mr. Gordon," she said sharply.

Mohammed poked his head around the door. "Missie?"

"A beer, please, Mohammed."

"Wim has a problem with a pump - says he'll be back around ten." Henderson sat on the arm of the couch and rested his hand on his thigh. "Thanks, Mohammed." He drank the beer in one long gulp. "Ah, that's better."

Frieda smiled politely, then turned her head: "Mohammed!" The dark face appeared. "Make something cold." He nodded.

"How's it going, now, Frieda?" Henderson asked.

She shrugged. "It's certainly not Bahrein - we had a house there, with things to do, places to go in the evening. This is - " She shook her head.

"You'll get used to it, Frieda, we all do." He slapped his thigh and laughed. "Anyway, you should come down to the pool more often. There's usually only Madge and Frances - if I get there early enough to dodge the Welsh Brigade. But I'd better be off, I'm going back to the plant tonight. While you're tucked up in bed I'll be x-raying welds. Tarra! Thanks for the beer."

She stood at the door and listened to his quiet footsteps on the stairs.

Wim came in at ten, tired and dirty, took a beer from the fridge and drank deeply from the can. He wiped his hand across his mouth. "Did Gordon come up?"

She nodded. "Nurul and Mohammed have gone. There's cold chicken salad, will that be alright?"

"Yeah, fine, I'm not hungry." He yawned. "I'm too tired to eat much."

She put the dish on the table then poured some wine. He sat heavily in the chair, toying with the glass. "God, I'm stoned tonight." He drank, then picked at the chicken.

She leant across and touched his arm, running her fingers through the fine hairs.

"What've you been doing today?" he asked.

She looked at him and smiled wanly. "Why do I always get stuck with Madge and Frances." She nudged his arm. "I wish I could spend a day, just one, going round some decent shops. I'd love to buy a few nice dresses and tops, just to feel ... well, a bit feminine again."

"What do you mean, again?"

"Can't you really see? Do you even care? I don't ever want to get like Madge ... we'll stop before then, won't we?"

He shook his head in amusement. "Shops! Dresses! I know the bazaar's not quite the Konigsallee, but still - come off it, Frieda!"

"Why did they build the plant here, in the middle of nowhere; three hours on that dreary train from Dacca."

"The plant is here, my dear Frieda, because -"

"Oh I hate how you say that, as if -"

"The plant is here because the natural gas it uses is here. It's as simple as that. "He wiped his fingers. "I know you're bored, but use your imagination - you're a graduate, for heaven's sake!"

"Undergraduate."

"OK, so I took you away from the bright lights of Dusseldorf. You want cases to study, look around - all these cooped-up neurotics just begging for your attention." His voice softened. "All I'm saying is that you don't have to be bored." He rose. "I'm going to have a shower, then into bed. I'm deadbeat."

"Do you mind if I go for a walk?" She slipped a cardigan around her shoulders.

He sighed. "I'm not your warder, you don't have to ask, just do it."

"I can't sleep, not yet. A bit of fresh air would -"

"That's fine, but you don't need to justify - you want a walk, go for one. I'll probably be in bed when you get back, so take a key." He scratched his chest then went yawning to the bathroom. As she closed the door she heard the water running.

It was a clear, starry night. Lightning flickered on the horizon as she approached the main gate and looked out at

the market stalls linked by a string of dancing lights which
cast the faces of the strolling villagers in and out of the
darkness.

"You OK, Missie?"

She jumped. "Oh hello, Mohammed, you startled me."

"Sorry, Missie, I was talking with my friend in the Mess.
I am going home, now, goodnight."

She watched as he went through the gate, nodded to the
guard, and mingled with the crowd. He lived in a shed
beyond the pond on the outskirts of the village. She turned
and followed the path along the compound fence, walking
between small, planted shrubs and palms. An owl screeched
high on an apartment verandah. She shivered, drew her
cardigan tight around her breast and walked back to the flat.

Wim was asleep, with the sheet down around his thighs.
Parting the mosquito net she lifted the sheet up over his
chest. As he snored softly into the pillow her lips twisted in
a thin smile. She poured a glass of milk from the fridge and
sat at the narrow table in the small kitchen and gazed
through the darkened window to the distant lights of the
plant.

The morning sun burned her shoulders as she lay at the
edge of the pool with a book in her lap, watching the boy in
his laundered white uniform sweep leaves from the tiled
path. Hearing the soft flip-flop of sandals she looked up,
shielding her eyes.

"Hi, Frieda!"

She caught a whiff of suntan lotion. "Oh, hello."

"I'm glad you took my advice. It's great to see you!"
Henderson knelt beside her, balancing on his toes. "Would
you like a whisky or vodka?"

"At ten in the morning?"

He laughed. "I suppose it is a bit early. A coke, then?"

"If you're going to the bar you could get me an orange."

"Sure, orange it is." His body was suddenly cast in
shadow. "Hello, girls," he said. "How are you this fine
morning? Anyone for orange?"

"Vodka and orange, Gordon, dear," said Frances,
plopping herself down on a basket chair.

He rose and stretched. "Same for you, Madge? ... of course."

Frances turned to Frieda, her eyes hard. "Sure looked cosy, just the two of you - didn't it, Madge?" She leant forward and gently squeezed Frieda's knee. "Fancy him, my dear?" She dabbed her nose and cheeks with suntan lotion and spread it lightly over her face.

Madge gave a tiny squeal of laughter. "Frances, will you stop embarrassing the girl!"

"Drinks, girls, drinks!"

Frieda sipped her orange, ice tinkling on the glass. Then she lay the glass by her side, opened her book and settled back on the li-lo.

"Be a dear, Gordon," said Frances, "do my back." She gave him the lotion and he began to rub in a slow circular movement up over her shoulder blades. She sighed with contentment. "That's good, round a bit ... aah!"

He shook his head in mock disgust, and glanced at Frieda. "I was talking to Wim this morning before coming off nightshift - says he's going to Chittagong tomorrow." He sighed. "Lucky devil!"

Frieda closed her book.

"Come on down with us to Dacca, next week, Gordon," said Frances. "Just Madge and me - we'll show you a thing or two!"

Madge laughed, coughing out smoke, and stubbed her cigarette on the tiles.

Adjusting her costume, Frieda closed her eyes. The sun covered her like a hot blanket.

At lunch she watched Wim eat in silence. When he left for the plant she went to the library. The small room was humid and stifling, and filled with the high pitched whine of mosquitoes. A pink, translucent gecko on the wall darted behind an old calendar. Tiredly, she leafed through a tattered *Der Speigel*, slapped a mosquito on her neck, then picked a paperback from the shelf, noted it in the register and returned to the flat.

At dinner she spooned her chicken soup, glancing at

Wim. "I was talking to Gordon Henderson this morning at the pool."

He looked up from his plate.

"Said you were going to Chittagong tomorrow."

Wim wiped his lips. "Did he, now. That was smart!"

"Why didn't you say?" she asked, her face suddenly flushed. "Surely I didn't have to find out from *him*?"

He shrugged, his eyes pale and expressionless. "I didn't want you upset."

"You could at least have mentioned it."

"Nothing was definite till this afternoon - it was on the cards, that's all. And I didn't really want to upset -" He paused, eyes searching her face. "Customs have been holding back a consignment for the plant: we need it now, and I'm the one who has to chase them."

"Can I come with you? I need to get away from here."

"I'll be running all over the docks, sorting out clerks and paperwork - you know what they're like. It could take all day, maybe longer. I'll be back Monday evening or Tuesday. It wouldn't be any joy for you stuck in a hotel or wandering around warehouses in this heat while I search for the right crate. You don't even know anyone in Chittagong!"

Mohammed came in from the kitchen. "Not now, Mohammed," she said. He backed away, his eyes nervously darting from one to the other.

"You'll find something to do," Wim said, reaching for her arm.

She shrank from him. "Madge and Frances?" She laughed. "Yes, I'll have plenty to do!"

"Have a night in the bar with -"

"It's the weekend, they've their men. Anyway, I'd rather stay here."

"Then why are you complaining?" He smiled. "As Gordon was so smart, suppose I ask him to take you into the village, look around the stalls - I know it's not the Ko, still... And you could see the video later at the club. What do you think?"

"You're not amusing."

"Don't you like our golden boy?"

She turned to the kitchen door. "Mohammed," she

called, brushing crumbs from the table, "You can bring in the main course, now." She swivelled back to Wim, her face stony. "It's Curry Madras, I hope you like it."

Next morning she stood with him on the embankment above the village, waiting for the train. Beyond the trees the red oxide painted bridge stretched across the broad mud-stained river.

A girl climbed up onto the embankment from the far side of the track, clutching a naked child. She wore a thin green sari which hung slackly on her body, exposing her breasts. She crossed the track and stood looking along the platform at the crowd waiting for the train, then placed the sleeping child on the ground and went back down the embankment. She knelt, lifting her sari, and urinated.

Frieda looked away, to the child curled, foetal, on the platform.

The girl returned, breaking into a toothless grin, and wandered along the platform, gazing up at the men.

Frieda nudged Wim. "Look at that child," she hissed angrily. "Anyone could step on him, left there like a piece of baggage!"

Wim shrugged. "She's rounding up business for tonight," he said. "These girls support themselves the only way they can."

She watched the girl weaving slowly in and out of the crowd.

"Twenty taka, that's the going rate. Two marks! That will keep her and her kid for another day."

With a roar from the crowd the train came clanking across the bridge. People were squatting on the roof, clinging to the sides. As it stopped the doors opened and a flood of men and saried women crossed the platform in waves of jostling humanity. Vendors pounced on captive passengers, balancing water jars, soft drinks, baskets of bananas and sticky sweets. It was chaos, Frieda thought, utter anarchy.

Wim gripped her hand tightly. "I'll see you Monday or Tuesday. Take care." He swung his bag through an open window of the first class compartment. "Take Missie home, now, Yousef."

The driver nodded. "Yes, boss."

"I'll wait till you leave," Frieda said, brushing a strand of damp hair from her forehead.

He gave her a hug, then boarded the carriage. She watched him squeeze through the crowd into the compartment, and settle at the window. As the train jerked into motion he gave a half smile and waved. "See you soon," he mouthed silently.

The train rounded the bend, leaving a track empty and shimmering in the morning heat. She turned and gazed down at the tiny houses and stalls; at the cinema covered in peeling posters. To the left of the village a small onion-domed mosque sat in a clump of trees. Farther off, a group of workmen squatting on the roof of a low concrete building were breaking bricks into rubble, keeping time to the beat of a drum.

The girl returned, glancing shyly at Frieda, then stood talking to an older woman. Her child lay as she had left him, curled up, motionless on the ground.

Frieda sighed. "Take me home, Yousef."

That evening she took a bath, then dried herself slowly, with care. She put on a robe, went through to the living room and poured a coffee then settled to listen to a tape. When the doorbell rang, she rose, annoyed that she had undressed so early, and went to the door, straightening her robe and peering quickly into the hall mirror. She opened the door.

"Oh, it's you, Gordon!" He stood leaning against the wall. "You know Wim's in Chittagong?"

"Yes, Frieda. Just thought perhaps you'd like company. Mind if I come in?" He edged onto the doorstep.

"Well ..." She swore inwardly. "Oh ... sorry, Gordon. Come in."

He sat on the couch, stretching his long legs out on the carpet.

"Would you like a coffee, or -?"

"Coffee's fine, Frieda." His eyes were bright, too bright

for her liking. "You have a nice flat." He reached out a hand to stop her. "No milk or sugar, just as it is." He looked around the room. "Better than the bachelor pads - all we have are four walls, bed, table and chairs."

She sat on the chair opposite.

"Good coffee." He cocked his head. "I like your tape. Doesn't it make you feel like dancing?"

She smiled nervously.

"It's a shame to waste it - you wouldn't like to dance?"

She laughed. "I don't think I'm quite dressed for dancing, do you?" She drew the robe tighter.

"Who's to see you? Come on." He held out his hand.

"Just drink your coffee, Gordon." She could smell the whisky on his breath.

"Come on!" He lifted her to her feet and pulled her close. "Shame to waste the music." He slipped both arms around her, and as they moved slowly she looked over his shoulder at the paintings Wim had bought in Dacca, the rows of tapes and books on the shelf. As he turned her round she saw that his eyes were closed, his face a stupid grin.

"Gordon ..." She pushed against him. "Gordon, please." He drew her to him, nestling his face against her hair, kissing the nape of her neck. "Gordon -" Her robe gaped open as she thrust him away. Angrily, she pulled it together. "Gordon, please go."

He looked down at her, his mouth distorted. "Come on, Frieda, enjoy yourself - I'm sure Wim is."

"Gordon -"

"Come on, Frieda!"

"Oh get out, just go."

She opened the door, and he stood looking at her, grinning.

"You don't really want me to go, do you?"

She pushed him out onto the landing. "Go home, Gordon, please."

She closed the door and pressed her head against it, listening as he went down the stairs. Then she gazed at her flushed face and shining eyes in the mirror, and smiled.

Into The Roots
Janice Galloway

I
t was raining and her hair was getting wet. Not a true
rain, but a drizzle, layering a blur on individual
strands, thickening into fat drops and sliding down to
the scalp. She could feel it there already, spreading
with the feel of insect feet. Her hair was flattening
with the weight, darkening under a dark sky from russet to
the vague amberblack of wood resin.

Alice's hair had always been excessive. Even the earliest
of her baby photos showed it, wee face struggling out from
under a heavy cloud. It had been white. She had been told
as much and could see in the pictures it was true; hair
matching the colour of the starched frills under the dazzle
of the studio lights. What was not part of a coxcomb strayed
out fuzzily as though the child had been plugged into an

electric socket or struck by lightening, accounting for the expression of boggle-eyed terror. No matter how hard she looked, it was impossible to detect eyebrows. She supposed they had been white too.

Ash, strawberry, ginger, red.

It got darker and it got longer. Through primary school, she carried the weight of its spinelength tangle, brushed, teased and woven into itself by her mother's efforts of will to a tightbound pleat. Still, it slipped the ribbon to blossom out behind as she ran, shrieking, in the playground. Evenings had been spent with head bent in contrition at the fireplace, clamped between mammy's knees as she tore out the knots and condemned them, spitting, to the flames. The longer it got, the more wayward it became. Enough was enough.

She had her first salon cut at the age of eleven: a new uniform and a new persona for the big school. She had been taken by the hand to Carrino's and given up to the dresser - mammy had other things to do. It crossed Alice's mind she was feart to watch. In the mirror, she saw the familiar coat retreat, open into a square of light, then cut from view as the door clicked across like a shutter. Alice was left gazing at her solitary self and was suddenly, thrillingly aware that this was the last of something. Last snapshot of childhood. She closed her eyes and heard the scissors slice.

Alice had known at the time, had said so, she would never forget the feeling the first incision had induced: as though her head were rising like a cork from the bottom of a sink of water. The dresser gave her the still-writhing pleat to hold: a thick-ended shaving brush petering away to elasticated nothing. She clutched it during the rest of the cutting as someone else emerged in the mirror. A long neck, very white from lack of sun, had grown up in the dark like a silent mushroom. The face was very pale and wee inside a curling auburn crop. They stood her up and dusted off the trimmings then handed her back. Mammy let her keep the pleat and she took it home to put into a shoebox; keeping it to take out every so often and remember who she had been. Then mammy started calling it *that thing*, brewing a distaste for the precious, matted snake-in-the-box, though when it disappeared, no one admitted having thrown it out. It didn't really matter: it was discovered only years later and by that time, the hair was long again.

That first cut triggered fresh growth. So much that within two years its mass had taken Carrino's so long to dress she had been late for the school dance. Slipping embarrassed and hair-sprayed into the squeaky gym-hall with its frenetic Grand Old Duke and illicit kisses. She was never a relaxed child but managed to join in. Enjoyed herself, too: looked well in her homesewn velvet and starched collar, but she went home alone. People couldn't see her eyes through the fringe and were suspicious. Alice liked it that way.

It brought its penalties, too. She remembered those interchangeable small boys who had chased and pulled her pigtail, hoping for a scream that she never gave. Bloodied her lip sometimes, caging in the pain with defiant teeth, determined not to let it show. And there had been a spider trapped in it once, a dark, struggling shape in the red mesh that shook her rigid with fear, numb for what to do. A boy again, this time one with the temerity to approach gently, had come to the rescue. He extricated both the spider and herself into their separate selves again without undue damage to either.

She folded her eyelids into a crease. Was it Charles? She supposed it must have been. Fourth year, so it was more than likely. That was the year she had dyed her hair for fun, two separate occasions and two colours, before letting it go its own way without further chemical intervention. The stripes of dye were visible if you looked hard enough, and he must have looked hard to get the spider. Long red stepladders, falling in fudgy bands of auburn from a straight white centre parting to well past her shoulderblades. They had all looked the same. She kept a sixth year photo: an avenue of senior girls with equiparted skulls and peaky faces aloof to the camera. She was there, right in the front row, fashionably sullen and mini-skirted; a leggy bookend with the girl closest. That other girl lived somewhere else now: two weans and no man. That would have wiped the smile off. As for the rest, Alice knew little or nothing; didn't keep up with old acquaintances. It was her mother had done that and it was an easy thing to take for granted when the woman was alive. Just a necessary part of the visits home, those tedious chants of births, marriages, turnsup for the books. Scandals. Till she became one herself and moved in with the man, living in sin in Charles' flat. Strange now she thought of it. She had never called it hers, for all her work and care there. Always Charles' flat or Charles' where she had swirled fair beard clippings from the sink, smoothed sheets, sewed neat cushions and learned to cook. She had never noticed at the time and now was too late.

She promised herself a haircut for the week she left - butcher the whole lot short because he had liked it long. But the break had dealt unkindly with her face and the thought of staring it out in a public mirror appalled her. She stayed in instead, putting paper on her own terrifying walls, in a place she would have to learn to call home. She tested smiles in the sheen of a clean bathroom sink, took pleasure from finding single strands of his blond in the weave of her jerseys. Kept finding them too, for a surprising length of time. Though now, sometimes, they weren't real.

Still raining. Misting down now and seeping across her head like melting syrup. Alice was becoming irritable. This was meaningless, mererly making it worse. What did she think she was doing out in this weather? Some idea to lift her depression, take a few photographs: the dull metal lump of the camera nuzzled cold into her palm in the folds of her pocket. The others were way in front. No, it wasn't helping: she was feeling no better and the continual smurr reinforced her suspicion that in walking alone, she was walking with a fool.

The backs of the people on the road ahead grew neither nearer nor further. One minute, she seemed to be gaining and the next they wavered like slipping frames of cine-film and were again inexplicably as far as before. Blurred vision - just another side-effect to make matters cloudier. Bloody pills. She wondered if she should force herself on, fight the cold denim cloy at her legs and catch up, as though she had fallen behind to tie a shoelace, admire the view. But she deflected the impulse easily. Own company was safest when these moods came.

The decision made her feel much better. Immediately, she stopped walking, stopped trying to make up lost ground and stood still in the middle of the road. Relief rubbed into her shoulders, at the base of her neck, warming affection for the disappearing figures ahead. Let them go.

And this was as it was meant to be. Alice stood and watched the familiar backs retreat as in a mirror. She closed her eyes and heard her heel twist in the gravel of the road; opened them. And there was the broken tree; split and blasted to the sky. Blood rushed to her lips as she smiled. It was a greeting. The tree waited. Alice stepped up onto the banking with one hand stretching and moist eyes. The tree glistened in the rain. Rich red and shrouded in grey. Mushrooming fungus spurted from all its orifices but one and that one she made towards. An eyesocket of a hole, with a swollen lip of bark and moss that only made the wound seem more raw. It would hurt, but had to be done. She steeled the muscles of her arm, flexing with the sound of metal swishing in her ears and cupped one hand, ready to receive.

Choking back her fear, Alice thrust out and plunged two clawed fingers into the hole. It was full of hair.

Clearing Out
Iain Hood

Mother died and I was forty-seven years old and hadn't cared for her or, now I realised, cared about her for quite a while. I was down on my luck, as they say, on the look-out for work down on the west coast and had found some labouring to do in Saltcoats. It had taken the lawyers a long time to track me down and by the time I knew she was gone she was long since buried and I was told almost straight away that there was no money and that even the money from the house would have to pay unsettled bills, including the funeral expenses. Seems like all they wanted me for was to clear out the house of her personal things, and that's why they came looking for me.

I wasn't going to bother and was going to let the council do it because there was nothing of hers that I wanted and because I couldn't afford to lose the wages. My landlady, the sour old maid, wanted to see some rent and I was working hard and trying not to think about drinking the hard earned cash and telling the sour old maid and the lawyers and Saltcoats and the whole world, in fact, where to go. But that's when I started thinking that maybe the old lady's stuff - some of it was good stuff - might be worth something. I went to see this antique dealer and convinced him it would be worth his while bringing me up to Glasgow to empty out the house, and even though I could tell by the way he was looking at me that all he saw was a bloated old drunk on the make, he decided that it would be worth it. He was just another guy on the make, after all. He would pick me up on Monday, when his shop was closed. He made me feel sick. He was one of those unsatisfied guys that even if you gave them a million pounds they still wouldn't find it enough. But then, like I say, judging him was judging myself, and vice versa for him, so we were going easy on each other. I'd always said I didn't care about money and that's how I'd ended up the way I had, scraping for a living every day and never comfortable. Except maybe on a barstool, half-cut. But I needed that money and by now it was myself that was making me sick.

I put it out of my mind and the trip up to Glasgow felt like nothing and passed quite quickly. We picked up keys from the lawyers' office in St. Vincent Street and when they saw me I was expecting them to ask for identification or something because their client had been so nice middle-class and I was such a scruff. We headed for the flat in Riddrie and there was some surprise waiting for us when we got there. The old lady had, by the looks of it, sold most of her stuff before she kicked the bucket and the place was nearly empty. The dealer looked really disappointed and I think I said sorry. Then again, maybe I just kept my mouth shut. He sort of walked around saying this was riddled with woodworm and that wasn't old enough and that it was a shame someone had got in there before him. Then we went into the room I remembered was her bedroom and there were some things on the floor. He seemed to like some of it and for a long time looked at some big china plate. He kept staring and saying how much he liked this tureen and the way he said tureen started to really annoy me. He said it like chureen, with a stupid gurgling sound in his throat. He said it over and over. He said it was a shame that the whole set wasn't left, that that would have been perfect. He put it down and started gesticulating. He said he wanted to be fair to me and could offer forty-eight, then he paused, no, he said, fifty quid for the lot.

For some reason, and I know I was being stupid, I said no, I wanted two hundred. He looked really shocked and said you're kidding and that he wasn't here to play games. He started whining about how he'd been promised a full house and how it was empty and it had hardly been worth his while coming. I said all right, I had been kidding and I'd take the fifty. It would have been half as much, he said, without that beautiful tureen.

I suddenly got this picture in my mind of my mother, in her coffin, decaying. And I saw me and this man as vultures picking her bones clean and dry and white and brittle, then as termites eating away at even these. We were leaving her without anything. But it was him who made a trade out of it. I had just made a terrible mistake. He was moving all the things he wanted together, bending over them.

That tureen cracked almost in half when I hit him, but that was nothing in comparison to his head. His brains came out onto the floor and there were clattering and thudding sounds as he fell into my mother's stuff. It's just that, I couldn't have stomached getting back into his car with him; not with my mother's last possessions in there too.

I stayed on in Glasgow, tramping the streets for quite a while, making some new friends. Everytime I was told to move on by the police I thought, how idiotic, I should be getting arrested. They did finally get me, and they thought I'd gone crazy the way I laughed when it happened.

But it was just that I'd finally worked out why everything had happened the way it had. A few days earlier I had been in the Underground at Buchanan Street on the platform that has no wall; has tracks on both sides. Without a wall to lean against you feel restless for something to happen, and I always feel scared and anxious that I might fall onto the tracks. Then the train had arrived and with it came a rush of stale, foul, empty air. That was exactly how my mother's empty house had smelled. That restless anxiousness - such a strangely empty feeling - was exactly how I had felt.

Forthcoming from Taranis Books

The Gringo Trees

By

J. William Doswell

Life in the small village of San Sebastian in El Salvador is poor, but not as bad as it could be. A living can be eked out from the seas and shorelines of the Pacific. Until, that is, the army is posted there to prevent campesinos from smuggling arms, with a devastating effect on the lives of the villagers.

> *Within six weeks, the substance of her life had been destroyed; all she considered meaningful and dear wiped out as completely as she could erase a mark in the sand. Why had God directed this fury at her? Had life not been hard enough?*
> *Below her a breeze flirted with the tops of the gringo trees. Their swaying fronds stirred memories and she lay back, eyes closed, and remembered.*

J. William Doswell is an American who lives in Virginia in the southern part of the United States. He has been a marine, a journalist, a political lobbyist and a member of the Central Intelligence Agency. Married with three grown sons, he now writes fiction full time.

The Gringo Trees £4.99 ISBN 1-873899-05-X

The Mating Of Dinosaurs

By

William Oliphant

This is the first full collection of poetry from one of Glasgow's most popular writers. Drawing on the best of limited edition booklets such as The Impact of Television on the Plumhead Parakeet, The Seamstress In The Nudist Camp and Devil's Dozen, as well as the many anthologies and magazines Oliphant has contributed to in the past, this volume is long overdue.

Born in 1920, William Oliphant left school at fourteen and worked in a variety of jobs servicing radio, television and electronic keyboard instruments. In the early fifties he was a member of Edward Scoullar's writers' group *The Wolves of Buchanan Street.* He had some success writing short fiction but gave up writing for a number of years to concentrate on bringing up his family. He began writing poetry in 1983.

The Mating Of Dinosaurs £5.95 ISBN 0-973899-10-6

WEST COAST MAGAZINE

All the stories you have read in this book were first published by West Coast Magazine. If you wish to read more fiction of this quality along with poetry, articles and reviews why not subscribe to the magazine?

West Coast Magazine ISSN 0963 - 732X

4 issues

UK   £8.00   inc P&P
Overseas   £12.00 inc P&P

Write to
West Coast Magazine/Media Bridge
PO BOX 849
Glasgow G31